PLANTANIMUS

PLANTANIMUS

REUNION

Joseph M. Armillas

iUniverse®

PLANTANIMUS - REUNION

iUniverse books may be ordered through booksellers or by contacting:

iUniverse
1663 Liberty Drive
Bloomington, IN 47403
www.iuniverse.com
1-800-Authors (1-800-288-4677)

ISBN: 978-1-5320-9528-3 (sc)
ISBN: 978-1-5320-9529-0 (e)

Print information available on the last page.

iUniverse rev. date: 02/13/2020

Table of Contents

ACKNOWLEDGEMENTS. vii

PROLOGUE ix

CHAPTER 1   Sulana Kay Meets Professor Artemus 1

CHAPTER 2   Thula's Visit. 25

CHAPTER 3   The Mansion in The Ranes Valley 40

CHAPTER 4   Remembrance 56

CHAPTER 5   Prognosis and Therapy For Sulana 69

CHAPTER 6   Test Inside Carlito's Mind 77

CHAPTER 7   Dinner and a Meditation 88

CHAPTER 8   Sulana Accepts Tarsia 98

CHAPTER 9   Rain and Salty Tears. 113

CHAPTER 10 Last Check Up 121

CHAPTER 11 One Last Conversation 127

CHAPTER 12 A Sister's Goodbye. 145

CHAPTER 13 "July 15th 3285" 147

CHAPTER 14 Alpha Sings for Sulana. 156

CHAPTER 15 A Warm Summer's Night. 170

ABOUT THE AUTHOR. 175

Acknowledgements

To Barbara Markay, My Heart and soul and to all women.
Cover Artwork by: Roman Cuilla Martinez
Samsara Wheel image by: Pixabay.com

Prologue

The story of Plantanimus "Awakening" begins in the 27th century in the year 2619, four hundred and eighty six years after the "Dark Period", an environmental holocaust that nearly wipes out the entire human race on Earth in the late 21st century.

After humanity's "2nd Renaissance" in the late 23rd century, mankind resumes the course of progress and eventually colonizes the Moon and Mars.

In the year 2485 a pandemic breaks out on Mars caused by a previously unknown virus in the ground water supply. The virus, called MV Recessive, kills every single adult on the planet but spares all Martian born children under the age of sixteen. Scientists eventually develop a genetically manipulated vaccine and inoculate the entire population of the solar system.

The pandemic brings about a conflict that culminates in a revolutionary war between the mother planet and its two territorial possessions, the Moon and Mars. As had occurred with colonies of patron nations on Earth many times in the past, Mars and the Moon eventually declare independence from the mother planet in the year 2486 and secede. The Moon and Mars become independent states and Earth has no choice but to grudgingly accept their independence.

A few decades after gaining its sovereignty, Mars becomes the industrial and technical powerhouse of the solar system, a situation that Earth resents. Unbeknownst to all, the MV Recessive vaccine causes a mutation in the DNA structure of the young Martian survivors of the pandemic. However the populations of Earth and the Moon are not similarly affected. The genetic mutation gives rise to a new generation of Martians with extraordinary abilities. From 2485 on, an unusual amount of psychically gifted children begin appearing in the Martian population. The average I.Q. of these children is unusually high.

PREVIOUSLY, IN BOOK 1, PLANTANIMUS "AWAKENING"

The main character of the story is Kelem Rogeston, a member of that generation of children born after the pandemic. He is a descendant of an illustrious family of Martian scientists and explorers that were instrumental in the colonization and development of Mars dating back to the 23rd century. In 2633, at age sixteen, Kelem is a genius with an immeasurable I.Q., already working on his doctorate in Interdimensional Physics and slowly becoming aware of his psychic powers.

Since the age of thirteen, Kelem has been experiencing a bizarre and unsettling recurring dream every night. In the dream he finds himself in a strange forest populated by enormous trees that tower several hundred meters above him. The trunks of these bizarre looking trees have golden bark and emit strange vibrations that sound like music. Searching for an answer to his problem, he seeks out famed physician and psychiatrist Professor Nicolas Alfano, one of Mars' eminent medical figures.

Nicolas Alfano is the leader of a secret but humane and ethical Martian society, called The Brotherhood of the Light. The Brotherhood is a one hundred and forty four year old organization made up of Martian psychics who formed the group more than a century before to protect Mars from the Phalanx, an evil, fascist society from Earth, bent on ruling the solar system under its fanatical right wing, authoritarian dogma. The organization now controls many aspects of the Terran government and plans to take over the planet and install one of their own as leader of Earth in order to accomplish their goals. One of the organization's main goals is to repossess Mars as a colony of Earth.

When Nicolas Alfano, a skilled mind reader meets sixteen-year old Kelem Rogeston, the future CEO of the Mars Mining Company, the largest most powerful corporation in the solar system, he realizes that Kelem is the most talented psychic that he's ever encountered. The boy is capable of sensing other people's emotions and can read minds at long distances.

A Martian prophet named Thorgen Kutmeier, also a member of The Brotherhood of the Light, has foretold of the coming of a new race of human beings many years before. He refers to these new humans as the Sixth Root Race. Nicolas Alfano is convinced that Kelem is the first member of that new race, the next step in the evolution of the human species. He takes Kelem under his wing to guide him and train him so that he can develop his psychic powers to their full potential.

A few months after Nicolas Alfano meets Kelem, a murder and theft is committed at the Stephen Hawking Center, a government sponsored scientific research facility on Mars that is the most advanced in the solar system. The scientists at the facility have been experimenting with a new technology called _n'time_. They have built a device designed to transport an object from a specific location in three-dimensional space, to other dimensions and back again to three-dimensional space, but at a different location. In theory, this interdimensional engine will allow mankind to travel a distance of several light years in mere hours, instead of centuries or even millennia.

Kelem becomes involved in the investigation by happenstance and due to his amazing intellect and psychic ability, he helps solve the murder and subsequent theft of the research data. He also prevents the destruction of a large part of Mars when he has a powerful dream in which he "sees" the Phalanx spy insert a virus in the Stephen Hawking Center's computer designed to cause the _n'time_ generator to self-destruct. Kelem skillfully disables the virus and the planet is saved. Later the authorities discover that the fascist Terran group is responsible for the attempt to steal the technology.

Afterwards he is invited to join the scientists at the Stephen Hawking Center as a member of the research team. He soon becomes the leader of the project and takes over the development of the technology, advancing its progress with amazing speed. Kelem eventually perfects the technology and designs an *n'time* ship capable of interstellar travel.

Soon after turning eighteen, Kelem finds love with Carlatta Del Mar, the beautiful and exotic daughter of the Terran ambassador to Mars, Don Francisco Del Mar. Their love affair is short lived when the Phalanx interferes and kidnaps Carlatta and her whole family and imprisons them on Earth.

After Kelem travels to Earth and fails to rescue Carlatta and her family from the clutches of the Phalanx, he returns to Mars and completes the construction of the solar Nations, the *n'time* ship that he designed. Together with a crew of one hundred, brokenhearted Kelem leaves Mars on the first voyage that will take humans beyond the confines of the solar system.

The ship meets with disaster and most of the crew perishes in a tragic accident, leaving Kelem and one of his best friends, Ndugu Nabole, stranded on Plantanimus, an Earth-like alien planet once ruled by a mighty race of humanoids, located many thousands of light years from the human solar system. On Plantanimus, he encounters the Dreamers, an ancient race of sentient plants that help Kelem expand his psychic powers and teach him the true nature of consciousness. The Dreamers are the same "trees" that Kelem has been dreaming about every night since his thirteenth birthday.

To ease his loneliness from the heartbreak of losing Carlatta Del Mar, the Dreamers create a part plant, part animal facsimile of her. At first Kelem rejects the "plantanimal" because she reminds him of the real Carlatta. But eventually Kelem accepts the facsimile who he names Anima and develops a platonic and spiritual relationship with her.

Six years after arriving on Plantanimus, an alien species (the Kren) land on Plantanimus. The Kren are an ancient and peaceful insect species who live in gigantic hive spaceships capable of faster than light travel. The Kren Queen Mother offers to return Kelem and Ndugu to Mars, their home planet.

Kelem is conflicted about leaving Plantanimus after growing so close to the Dreamers and Anima but decides to go back to Mars to bear witness for his friend Ndugu who, being a former Terran, could be blamed for the fate of the Solar Nations expedition if he returns without Kelem.

Promising to return someday Kelem leaves with a heavy heart hoping that the Kren will be able to return him to Plantanimus, the place that has become his real home.

PREVIOUSLY, IN BOOK 2, PLANTANIMUS "RETURN TO MARS"

Kelem and Ndugu Nabole return to the solar system courtesy of the Kren. Harry, the insectoid that the queen mother assigned to take Kelem and Ndugu back to Mars, will remain awake instead of hibernating, which is their custom, in order to keep the two men entertained during the twelve months that it will take to arrive at the human solar system.

When Kelem and Ndugu return to Mars, they discover that they're fifteen years out of sync with the timeline in the solar system. To their dismay they find that it's been twenty-one years since they departed in the ill-fated ship, the Solar Nations, in the year 2638. Kelem theorizes that the explosion that damaged the _n'time_ generator and killed most of the crew on the ship, must have pushed the ship forward in time by fifteen years. The current date is 2659!

As they make their way toward Mars, they're further shocked to learn that the hated Phalanx has taken over Earth's government and that Mars is once again a colony of the mother planet.

Kelem suggests to Ndugu that they return to Plantanimus but his friend refuses, claiming that he'd rather face the Phalanx than go back to the alien planet. They halt their journey to Mars and assume orbit around one of Saturn's moons to think about their next step.

While in orbit around the moon, they are captured by a strange group of Martians, claiming to be rebels fighting against the Terran forces. They are beaten and imprisoned by the rebels, accused of being Terran spies. Ndugu, originally from Earth is immediately suspect and after six years of living under Plantanimus' heavier than Earth's gravity, Kelem now looks like an earthman.

After a violent struggle in the rebel ship, in which Kelem and Ndugu help eliminate a psychotic member of the rebel ship who was threatening to take over the vessel and kill the captain and his family, Kelem and Ndugu are accepted as Martian patriots.

Afterwards, Kelem finds out that Mars has become a slave nation, forced to manufacture goods and technology for their Terran oppressors. The Phalanx rules the planet with an iron fist and Martians are slowly being worked and starved to death. His beloved Uncle Nardo and Aunt Maggie have been murdered by the Phalanx and the Brotherhood of the Light is on the run, hiding amongst the Martian population.

The rebel fleet has been on the run for fifteen years and their ships are falling to pieces. It won't be long before the entire rebel fleet, which is composed mostly of old and dilapidated Martian mining vessels, ceases to exist. Something has to be done and Kelem decides to be the one to take on the Terrans and the Phalanx and liberate his home planet.

He sneaks back to Mars to seek out the Brotherhood of the Light, knowing that if he can regroup the organization, the Martians will have a decent chance to repel the Terrans and regain their independence. With his enhanced mental and psychic abilities, Kelem slowly begins to turn things around and becomes the leader of the Martian resistance.

He liberates his friend and mentor, Professor Nicolas Alfano, who was the leader of the Brotherhood of the Light and who has been a prisoner of the Phalanx for close to sixteen years. Together, they put the Brotherhood of the Light back together and slowly begin to make progress in regaining Mars' independence. Through the miracle of the Quantum tide, the place where time and space do not exist, the Dreamers teach Kelem how to raise the spirits of the Martian rebels.

For six months, Kelem fights against the Black Guards, the Phalanx secret police, run by Soltan Voltanieu, the evil leader of the Phalanx and the individual responsible for the invasion of Mars and the subjugation of its people. He also has to contend with his stepson, Jude Voltanieu, who is a powerful psychic who has killed and tortured many Martians to do his stepfather's bidding.

Six months after returning to the solar system, Kelem comes back to the rebel fleet with a hijacked ship full of weapons and supplies and begins arming and rebuilding the rebels to face the mighty Terran Space Navy. He returns to Harry the Kren's ship, hiding behind a planetoid on the outer edges of the solar system, and asks for his help in the struggle. The alien agrees to help Kelem and the rebels with Kren technology that gives the Martians an advantage during the many battles soon to come.

After nine months of struggle, and several epic space battles, the Martian rebels succeed in liberating their own planet and defeat the Terran Space Navy while capturing many of their war ships.

Mars is now free but at a terrible cost. The planet has been decimated with civilian loses in the hundreds of thousands. During the struggle, Kelem has lost his childhood friend Billy Chong and many others close to him.

The Martians now ask Kelem to lead the newly formed Martian space armada to Earth, now practically defenseless after their defeat, to wreak havoc on the people of Earth.

Kelem pleads with the rebels and the people of Mars, not to take revenge against their human cousins and fortunately prevails. He knows that if the Martians do to the Terrans what the Terrans did to them, the solar system will never be free of war and strife. To the disappointment of many, Kelem resigns as the leader of the rebels and leaves Mars never to return.

He joins Harry the Kren in his ship and the alien surprises him by announcing that Harry is actually Harriet. The Kren, who has morphed into a female, is to be the Queen Mother of a new generation of Kren. Harriett takes Kelem back to Plantanimus, where he rejoins the Dreamers and his beloved Anima. Kelem dies of natural causes at the amazing age of one hundred and ninety-eight, leaving his beloved Anima and the Dreamers alone on Plantanimus once again.

In the year 2794, one hundred and twenty-eight years after the end of that war, a human space ship, the "Solar Nations II", makes contact with a humanoid species called the Tarsians.

The encounter with the Tarsians begins a new era in human history. Within a short time, humans and Tarsians are trading goods between their two worlds. The Tarsians are not as advanced as humans, though they have space travel technology. The Tarsian Empire, ruled by a constitutional monarchy, is a conglomeration of over thirty planets located nine hundred light years from Earth.

The Tarsians are excellent craftsmen and their art and luxury items are like nothing humans have ever seen. In turn, the Tarsians are amazed by *n'time* technology and all the other scientific advances that humanity has made. Fortunes are quickly made from the import and export of goods and technology, and the two civilizations soon become dependent on each other's economies.

But in 2804, the Tarsians are invaded by an unknown species called the Gulax. The Gulax are a reptilian warrior race bent on conquering the galaxy and they begin invading Tarsian worlds one after the other.

The Solar System Government decides to come to the aid of the Tarsians to protect the economy of both civilizations and to prevent being conquered by the Gulax in the future. At first, the humans and the Tarsians succeed in repelling the Gulax. But the Gulax eventually strike back and retake even more territory. Now, in the year 2834 the War has been going on for thirty years, and the alliance is losing to the Gulax.

Previously in book 3, The Gulax War

The third book in the trilogy tells the story of Alexei Rogeston a descendant of the legendary genius and psychic Kelem Rogeston. Alexei is a military commander fighting for the Human-Tarsian Allied Forces against the Gulax, an alien reptile species intent on conquering the galaxy. Alexei discovers a plot to undermine the Alliance and joins forces with the beautiful and exotic Princess Kani, daughter of King Velmador, ruler of the Tarsian Empire.

The war is not going well for the Alliance and Alexei and Kani fight against spies, cultural prejudice and the Gulax and eventually succeed in bringing the 30 year war to a peaceful end. Unbeknownst to them, destiny has more surprises for duo when the Kren, a peaceful insect species rescue them from a near fatal space ship wreck and take them to Plantanimus to meet Kelem Rogeston, Anima and the Dreamers, the sentient psychic Plantanimals that helped Kelem Rogeston liberate Mars from the tyranny of The Phalanx 186 years before.

CHAPTER 1

Sulana Kay Meets Professor Artemus

Sulana Kay, a young Gulax female was led into Professor Artemus's office by a very pretty Tarsian student. "The professor will be with you shortly," she said in a strange tone of voice, pointing to a single leather upholstered chair facing a large ornate wooden desk.

The girl left the room closing the door. Her steps faded quickly as she walked away.

The Gulax sat down on the chair and carefully scanned the office taking in the layout of the rectangular room. Three of the walls had floor to ceiling bookcases replete with ancient tomes written in several galactic languages some of which she had never heard of before. She hadn't seen that many printed books all in one place in her entire life. She wondered where the professor kept his 'opto-readers'.

On the wall behind a finely carved oak desk, an ancient grandfather clock marked time in the old style Terran system. It's mechanism tick-tocking sixty times per cycle. To her sensitive Gulax ears the sound from the old contraption seemed disproportionately loud in the quiet room. Having grown up on Terra Prime she knew what this relic was and smiled at the fact that few if any on this quadrant of space would know what a 'grandfather clock' was.

She stuck out her tongue and 'smelled' the molecular decay of the various organic enzymes and materials that these books were made of. Some were familiar to her. Many were truly foreign and strange.

The room 'smelled' old and musty. Still, there was something vaguely comforting and relaxing about this room. She could tell that the furniture was made of real wood and not faux material, which was typical these days, particularly in Centralia which sat near the center of the Milky Way Galaxy about 600 parsecs from Terra Prime. She suspected that it must have cost a small fortune to transport these antiques all the way from Earth to here. She couldn't help but wonder how a university scholar like Professor Artemus could afford to surround himself with so many priceless antiques.

She turned and faced the fourth wall dominated by three large Terran medieval period style windows, covered in some sort of stained glass panels depicting scenes from earth's ancient past. She thought that they might be religious in nature but she wasn't sure.

The place was straight out of a museum display. She guessed that the style of décor was from the late 19th century Victorian era. She looked around to see if there were any 33rd century devices in the room but every object down to the primitive pen and ink set in the middle of the desk appeared to be period specific. Maybe the old man was a freak for all things ancient.

Beyond the windows, through the slightly distorted antique glass panels, she could see the main plaza of Centralia University surrounded by the hyper modernistic architecture of the campus buildings. She decided that the contrast between the two time periods would make an interesting photo if taken from the rear wall of the room, thereby encompassing the old and the new in one image.

She glanced at the wrist comp on her right hand and noticed that a twelfth of an hour had passed since she entered the room and wondered how much longer she'd have to wait until the professor arrived. She felt impatience building up in her. Perhaps Zephron Artemus was avoiding her. She'd been trying to get an appointment with the famous professor for several weeks now and just yesterday she'd been notified at her hotel that he would meet with her today.

Her research on ancient history had brought her to Centralia, now the hub of the galaxy in intellectual advancement and commerce. Long ago Tarsia Prime and Terra had been the center of civilization but their location at the edge of the Milky Way made those two planets too distant from the main group of new worlds where various new alien species and new nation states had been discovered and contacted in the late 28th century.

Even Plantanimus, once the spiritual center for many people, had seen better days. Relegated now to a second-rate tourist attraction visited mainly by college students on holiday and the few believers who were still members of the dwindling Church of St. Kelem. She reflected with some sadness how the bodies of the once mighty Dreamers now preserved and displayed on Mount Olympus like the bones of ancient dinosaurs in a museum, were but a mere curiosity to the uninformed visitors of today who have but the vaguest idea of the true significance of their place in history.

Once they were the givers of new life to the sick and dying. But in the late 29th the demand for life prolongation eventually became too severe. Plantanimus could not accommodate the huge amount of people who came seeking immortality and soon war came to Plantanimus. The competing adversaries surrounded the planet and a blockade was put in place by all the planets involved in the conflict, thus preventing each other from using Plantanimus.

The tense blockade lasted thirty six years during which many battles and skirmishes broke out around Plantanimus. On more than one occasion a few of the Dreamers were damaged and a few perished, but fortunately most were able to persevere despite the turmoil.

It was near the end of this thirty six year period when all-out war seemed almost impossible to avoid, and the destruction of Plantanimus and the Dreamers all but guaranteed, that Tatiana Rogeston (then one hundred and six years old) announced to all involved that she had developed a new and easily applied therapy that did not involve the contribution of the Dreamers. She had discovered a way to prolong life for the millions who were clamoring to live beyond their years.

At first no one believed her, but she proved her claims and then astoundingly, she freely gave the technology to anyone who wanted it. Within a year, the blockade around Plantanimus was ended and as time passed by, and with the issue of death becoming almost a voluntary decision by everyone who received the therapy, the planet lost its value to the outsiders.

After that, only very high-minded spiritual seekers among the then, eleven known races, continued coming to Plantanimus to commune with the Dreamers, or take spiritual counsel from Kelem, Animah and Tatiana Rogeston.

In the year 2912 an exo-botanist from a planet called Garuinne doing research on the flora of Plantanimus, published a galaxy wide report stating that the Dreamers were slowly dying. Only those who were alive during the heyday of Plantanimus paid any attention to the announcement. For the rest of the billions upon billions of inhabitants on the newly discovered planets now numbering more than eighty, the news was all but ignored.

A few members of the galactic press showed up in Kehrrum, the old capital of Plantanimus a month later to interview all the Plantanimals still living on the planet as well as the Rogestons to find out if the rumors were true. They were met by Renato Rogeston, a young man claiming to be the son of Gutan Rogeston, the oldest son of Alexei and Kani Rogeston.

Renato confirmed the fact that the Dreamers were indeed dying of old age after nearly eleven thousand years of existence and that within half a century, the Dreamers and all the Plantanimals that they'd help create, would all be gone. When the press asked to be taken to Mount Olympus to take photos of the dying Dreamers, the Plantanimal colony and the legendary homes of the Rogeston family, Renato regretfully informed them that the family and the colony were in deep prayer and meditation to prepare for the inevitable end. He also announced that the planet would be off limits to all but a few select individuals for the foreseeable future until all had passed on.

Five decades later the only sentient plants to have ever lived anywhere in the galaxy had all died. Their massive bodies still stand to this day, preserved expertly by nature conservationists. Plantanimus was eventually declared a "historic site planet" by the newly formed Galactic Council and in 2995, an organization called The Plantanimus Conglomerate, took over the management of the planet and a within a

4

few years, Plantanimus became a popular vacation site for young college age students, history buffs and pilgrims of the Church of St. Kelem.

After that, Plantanimus faded into the fog of history. Little is known of the fate of the many individuals that the Dreamers helped transition into Plantanimal bodies including Kelem, Animah, Alexei, Kani, Tatiana et al. Most historians assume that all other members of the Rogeston clan who had transitioned into Plantanimals, died along with the last of the Dreamers as well. And it is believed that all the members of the family who were living in humanoid form at that time, departed the planet to points unknown sometime around 2980.

The Rogeston Compound located at the mouth of the Tikset Delta is one of the most popular sites on the planet with actors impersonating the various members of the Rogeston clan for visiting tourists.

Sulana, a graduate student from the University of South Africa on Terra Prime, had been working on her dissertation for her PHD in History of the Plantanimus Period for two years. In the process of researching the period she became fascinated with the saga of the Rogeston family and their connection to the Dreamers and their effect on the history of the galaxy.

Rather than writing a generalized treatment of the period, she decided to focus on the more interesting and challenging Rogeston connection to Plantanimus and the Dreamers. But she had run into a dead end regarding the fate of the Rogeston clan at the end of the 30th century. She looked for a long time for historical records of the Rogestons following that period, but no records of any kind could be found. It was as if the family had vanished into thin air. Knowing that it was impossible for a family of some two hundred people, (according to accounts of individuals who had lived on Plantanimus prior to 2965) to completely leave no trail or evidence of their existence, Sulana came to believe that the Rogestons had purposely gone into hiding.

She couldn't imagine why such an illustrious family would suddenly and inexplicably exclude themselves from history as if they never existed. She knew that there had to be good reason for it all, and she became obsessed with solving the mystery.

Then three months ago while vacationing with her parents in Montevideo, in old South America, she had come across an obscure little book written by the notorious genius historian, Zephron Artemus, titled; "The Infinity Poems of Zeus the Dreamer".

It was the title and the unusual content that drew her attention to the publication. That, and the fact that it was written by the foremost scholar of history in the known galaxy.

The book contained ten very long poems purportedly composed by Zeus, the oldest of the Plantanimus Dreamers and translated into standard galactic and edited by Artemus himself. Each poem was several pages long and full of the flowery language of the Dreamers. Sulana read each and every word of the sometimes-rambling prose, much of which didn't make any sense to her methodical and disciplined Gulax mind, but she muddled through.

But then, on the tenth and final poem she came across a very unusual stanza:

> *In my transcendental dreaming mind, I feel the joy*
> *of the betrothed pair*
> *A child of Kani drinks the wedding wine and sings a*
> *song of love so fair*
> *Though distance keep my empty hands aside*
> *I feel each one of you through the quantum tide*
> *My human eyes now shedding newborn tears*
> *Give thanks to Tiana for these welcomed years*
> *For without her this new life would never be*
> *Still of movement and blind of eye I'd be*

Sulana read this over and over again and interpreted the stanza to mean that Zeus was referring to his 'body' as somehow being human and possessing eyes and shedding tears as a new experience and most interestingly, thanking Tiana (which could be a short form of Tatiana) for his new life.

Still further on, an even more curious section read:

My home of eons left behind, I know not where I'll be in time
A newborn life takes its first breath, I've left the ground and cheated death
I move to where I set my mind, I walk a path it feels sublime!
Old life and body now are spent, I leave this place where once I dreamt

This read as a statement of rebirth or renewal or perhaps of transitioning to a new form of life, one that possessed arms, legs etc. in other words, a humanoid form. The idea seemed ludicrous even to consider, but despite Sulana's logical Gulax mind, the possibility had its merits.

Her curiosity about the publication was peaked further by the fact that nowhere in its pages did the book specify where the good professor acquired his source material. In addition, she could not find any other publication that alluded to any known collection of Dreamer poetry anywhere in the galaxy. Either the distinguished Zephron Artemus had in his possession a number of unknown manuscripts concerning the Dreamers that no one knew anything about, or he had a secret and intimate connection with the Rogestons, or, he had made the whole thing up in an untypical surge of literary creativity.

Sulana had read many of his books during her research for her dissertation, particularly "The Rogeston Dynasty", his "Biography of Kelem Rogeston" which was considered the most complete and accurate ever published, and last, and perhaps the most significant piece of the trilogy, "History of Plantanimus, Genesis of the Dreamers". Although the man was the foremost authority on all things Rogeston, Plantanimus and the Dreamers, his writing style was very factual and devoid of any flowery language. She seriously doubted that "The Infinity Poems of Zeus the Dreamer" was his own creation.

He'd also written many other books about exo-anthropology, religion and philosophy, and several treatises on intergalactic politics and future trends. The man held more than seven PhD's in other disciplines as well.

Fifty six major books in all. Sulana wondered how the good 'Doctor' had managed to write so many important publications in his fifty-six years of life, while managing to receive so many doctorates.

It took her one and a half months of investigation to locate the man and find out that he held a permanent position at Centralia University as dean of Antiquity Studies and History Department. And another month to get an appointment with him, and then two weeks in a Tareen transport (the only vessel that she could book at the last minute) to reach Centralia. And finally, two boring weeks waiting at her hotel for a call from the professor's secretary, letting her know that the professor finally had time to meet with her.

To make matters worse, winter was but a few weeks away and the decreasing temperature in Centralia was already making Sulana uncomfortable. She had already come to the realization that the sight of a Gulax in the planet's capital was an unwelcome sight to many of the races that lived on this world. So, she had spent most of the time holed up in her hotel room with the thermostat turned to high, and only coming out of her room when it was absolutely necessary.

Today the temperature had risen to 69 degrees Fahrenheit but she still felt cold. "Being part lizard has its downside," she said to herself in jest.

In the midst of her reverie her delicate ears picked up the sound of heavy steps in the hallway. "Definitely male", she thought.

The door opened and in walked Professor Artemus.

Sulana jumped to her feet somewhat clumsily.

The Gulax face does not have muscles that express surprise like humans do, but to anyone that's been around Gulax long enough, it would have been clear that Sulana was taken aback by the physical appearance of Zephron Artemus. Her ears instinctively pulled back and flattened against her skull, if only for an instant.

The tall thin man with jet black curly hair and clear blue eyes now closing the door and walking towards her with a smile on his face, looked to be in his mid-twenties. For a moment, she was sure she'd seen him somewhere before, but couldn't place when or where it was that she might have met him, yet, there was something very familiar about him.

"Sulana Kay?" he said in a smooth pleasant voice, as he reached for her gloved hand.

"Professor I'm so glad to finally meet you", she responded shaking his hand.

"I'm so sorry to have kept you waiting all this time Ms. Kay, but we're about to start our winter trimester and I've been rather busy these past few weeks. I hope that you've had a pleasant time here in Centralia while waiting to see me."

He rounded the desk and motioned with his right hand for her to sit back on the leather chair as he sat on his.

"I've managed," answered Sulana, politely.

He looked out the window and then at her gloved hands. "May I raise the temperature to make you more comfortable Ms. Kay?" he asked, knowing that her cold-blooded metabolism could use the warmth.

"Oh, please don't bother on my account professor, I'll be just fine with the room as is."

"Nonsense Ms. Kay. I've lived among your people and I know that you'd feel much better around 85 degrees Fahrenheit. May I offer you a hot drink, perhaps a green tea?

"Yes, that would be ideal for me, thank you."

The professor brought his index finger to his right temple and pressed lightly. "Thula, please bring us two green teas".

"You have an audio implant," observed Sulana.

"Yes, and I've had a corneal visual data interface put in both my eyes as well. I got tired of losing opto-readers and personal comps. Now all I need to carry with me is this," he said, pointing to a small flat metal disk on his left earlobe.

"Your hard drive?" she asked looking at the silver earring.

"Yes, it can hold several Petabyte's worth of information, far more than I'll ever use in my entire lifetime."

"No wonder there are no com technology devices in the room, the man's wired for audio video and data!" she realized.

"Any side effects from all that technology in your head?" she asked casually.

"Only an occasional glitch in my field of vision now and then, and only when I'm working with very large images, but nothing so far that would compel me to have the stuff taken out."

"How long have you had the implants in?" she inquired further.

"Several years now. You see I'm a victim of my own success." he said, smiling. "I published my first book when I was twelve years old and then when I turned thirteen, I wrote three books that year. Ever since then, my publishers expect a minimum of three new manuscripts every year."

"How do you find the time to do anything but do research and write?" she asked in wonder.

"Oh well, you see, I hardly ever sleep. I take two ninety minute naps every day, one at three pm and another one at eleven pm. I plan to slow down a little in the next few years." he added, almost apologetically. "I'm not as young as I used to be."

"Forgive me professor but you don't look a day older than twenty five in Terran Years."

Zephron Artemus laughed softly and then leaned back in his chair a little. "That is why I don't allow my photo or any facsimile of my appearance to be printed or included in any of my publications. As a matter of fact, I don't allow anyone to record an image of me at any time, and that includes my own family."

"I always wondered about the fact that I couldn't find any photos of you," she stated, looking at him. "I must admit that when you walked in, I was taken aback by your appearance. I was expecting to meet a very scholarly looking human in his late fifties."

"Precisely!" he exclaimed. "One would think that in this day and age, the halls of academia would be populated by beings fully capable of accepting the genius and expertise of a learned colleague, regardless of his age, gender, race or appearance, but you'd be wrong."

"I must plead guilty to my own prejudice. I guess I've been living among humans for too long," Sulana added, smiling, realizing that he'd very skillfully avoided talking about his age.

"Please, Ms. Kay, I didn't mean to criticize you in any way. I was making a general comment about the nature of intellectual beings. As a matter of fact, I must confess that when I received your first communiqué, I was somewhat surprised to find out that a Gulax female had decided to make the study of galactic history her life's work."

"Please call me Sulana professor. And yes, it is highly unusual for a Gulax, and particularly a female Gulax, to go into any career other than technology or the military. But fortunately, my parents are untypical Gulax themselves, though both are planetologists by training. My parents and I are descendants of the first wave of Gulax immigrants to arrive on Terra a few decades after the end of the Gulax War. They grew up on Earth as I did. My mother's hobby is painting beautiful desert scenes and she regularly travels to Cairo to sell her artwork at an annual art fair. In his spare time, my father runs a small kennel in Johannesburg where he raises South African Boerboels a breed of large dogs that he sells all over the quadrant. All very un-Gulax behavior as you can see."

"An artistic mother and a dog breeder father, hmm," mused the professor. "Are your parents considered weird within the Gulax community back on Earth?"

"Not at all. You see, Earth born raised lizards," she said, using the Terran slang for her species, "are quite different than those born on Gulax Prime. Besides, back on Earth, our species is so intermingled with native humans that our presence is hardly noticed," she paused for a moment, carefully choosing her next words. "I can't say the same for Centralia."

"I can imagine the looks you must be getting around town. You are probably the only live Gulax anyone has ever seen on this planet."

"Yes," Sulana agreed. "Your secretary seems to be one of them. Although her strange attitude toward me is most likely curiosity." She paused and looked at the professor to see his reaction. "She kept staring at me and would avert her eyes whenever I caught her looking at me. I found it most interesting," Sulana mused casually.

Professor Artemus was about to respond to Sulana's statement, when light footsteps approaching the room could be heard in the hallway.

The professor got up from his chair, opened the door and let Thula, the strange Tarsian assistant in. She entered with a silver tray in her hands, carrying two large steaming mugs which she put on the desk. Perhaps because she was in front of the professor this time, the Tarsian girl smiled sweetly at Sulana, then curtsied slightly and promptly left the room.

The green tea smelled sweet and pungent. Sulana reached for her cup and drank slowly, closing her eyes as the hot liquid warmed her from the inside out. The room was also getting warmer now and Sulana felt comfortable enough to take her gloves off.

The professor leaned back in his chair and looked at Sulana intently. She in turn, stared back at him with her unblinking reptilian eyes. After a short while, both changed their gaze to avoid an awkward moment.

Now that she had been in his presence for a while, she noticed that although his body looked so very young for a man his age, his eyes had the depth and intensity of a much older person. "Perhaps he's had a rejuvenation procedure done even though he's only in his fifties. Or perhaps, it's the corneal implants that make him look that way." She wondered how he'd react if she were to ask him about his chronological age.

"I'm curious to find out," said the professor, interrupting her train of thought. "Why a graduate student from Terra prime would come all the way to Centralia from the edge of the galaxy to talk to me about the Rogestons. I know you're trying to finish your dissertation and I would love to help you in any way I can. But as I've already explained in my correspondence to you, everything I know on the subject, has already been published and is a matter of public record."

"Yes I know that, but I've run into a dead end regarding the fate of the Rogeston clan at the end of the 30th. and I thought that perhaps, since you wrote the Rogeston/Plantanimus trilogy early in your career, I hope to find find something in your notes that could provide some leads for my own research. Perhaps, something that you missed, since none of your books were meant to delve into the Rogeston family history beyond 2965. I hope I can compel you to let me review your original research and materials. And of course." she added, earnestly, "I would fully credit you for any data that I glean from your work."

The professor leaned back in his chair staring at the ceiling and rubbed his chin pensively. After a long pause he spoke. "I don't have any objection to giving you access to all my research although I doubt that you'll find anything useful."

"For my sake, professor I hope you're wrong," answered Sulana, relieved at being able to access the professor's information.

"Why are you so keen to know the fate of the Rogestons?" asked the professor, looking at Sulana quizzically. "After all, once Tatiana developed the technology for life prolongation, she and the rest of the family made it plain to the rest of the world that they wanted to be left alone. And besides, what would be accomplished by seeking them out? Perhaps their descendants don't want to be found as well."

Sulana looked down at the floor for a while and then spoke passionately. "Doesn't it bother you that a family whose members have been so instrumental in the history of the galaxy beginning with Terra's "Dark Period" more than a twelve hundred years ago, have been so thoroughly forgotten by historians, scholars and the world at large?"

"For my part yes, since I've obviously written the three best known books that detail the history surrounding the Rogeston name. But on the other hand, Sulana, there are many other notable individuals and families that are just as important to the history of the galaxy as the Rogestons, such as the Davian kings of the Tareen. Let's not forget that they opened the doors for Terrans and Tarsians to the rest of the galaxy. Without them, Humans, Tarsians and Gulax would still be searching for intelligent life in our little corner of the Milky Way. And then, what about the Kren? Without them, Kelem Rogeston would have been just a footnote in Earth's history and the Dreamers would have never been heard of."

"Quite true professor. The truth is that I could turn in my manuscript right now if I wished. After all, it's four hundred pages detail the Rogeston era quite well, and it is the original purpose of my work." Then Sulana paused, searching for the right words to say. "However, some instinct in me compels me to go forward and seek the answer to the mystery. I've become somewhat obsessive-compulsive about the subject I'm afraid." Sulana wondered if she should tell the professor how her obsession with the Rogestons had driven her to the point of breaking the law, but she'd wait to reveal that fact once she'd known him better.

"You certainly don't fit the personality profile of a stereotypical Gulax Sulana!" remarked the professor. "Your preoccupation with this issue is positively human in nature. You are a most interesting lizard."

"Thank you, professor I've always been an 'odd duck' if you know the expression."

"Even though I was born and raised on New Lavonia, I'm quite familiar with Terran slang," the professor answered with a laugh. "I hope you'll decide to stay in Centralia while you complete your research. I would like to get to know you better as a person, and I have a feeling that we can learn a few things from each other," he added, with a warm and friendly expression.

"Thank you, professor. Unfortunately, my finances will not allow me to remain in Centralia much longer. As you know, I've been in the capital for two weeks now while waiting to see you and I'm sure that you are aware that there are no cheap hotels on this entire planet."

"First, I want to apologize once again for making you wait for so long. And second, I must plead ignorance regarding the cost of living here in Centralia or anywhere else for that matter. My living expenses are handled by a management company and I'm blissfully ignorant of money matters by choice. I realized early on in my career, that for me to be able to do my work without the pressures of everyday living, I had to give control of such mundane distractions to other people. However, having said that, I know that I'm wealthy enough to provide food and lodging for you for an indefinite amount of time here on Centralia. And I will not take no for an answer."

Sulana didn't have to think about the offer for more than a second or two. But she made the effort to appear to be mentally debating whether to accept or not for a few seconds more. She would accept his offer immediately and agree to stay in Centralia for as long as it would take for her to finish her research. Besides, she needed time to wait for the right moment to bring up the issue of the Dreamer poetry book and discover Zephron Artemus' true connection to it.

"I'm honored by your invitation Professor Artemus and I will take your word that you truly are rich enough to provide me with a place to stay at no detriment to you. I too would like to get to know you better, and nothing would please me more than to spend time getting to know the illustrious Zephron Artemus."

"Good, we are agreed," he said. Then, after pausing and touching his left temple, he began talking to an unseen person. "Waldo, please bring my flier to the roof of the history building. I have a guest that needs to go back to the city to pick up her luggage. By the time you get to her hotel, I'll have a new location for you to take her to. By the way, I want the cabin temperature to be set to 90 degrees Fahrenheit for her comfort. Is that understood?" The professor looked at the wall of books across from his desk as he listened to the voice in his head for a short while, and then he touched his temple again.

"Thank you for providing your flier to shuttle me around but won't the 90 degree temperature be uncomfortable for your pilot?

"Not at all. You see, the thing has a separate cabin for the passengers."

"It must be a big flier!" Sulana responded, impressed.

"As I said," the professor added casually, "I am a wealthy man."

"Thank you professor. I am grateful beyond words."

"By the way," the professor said, getting up from his chair. "I forgot to ask you. You're not averse to flying, are you?" Sulana responded by shaking her head. Good! And do you prefer a ground floor or a higher story for your accommodations?"

"I don't have any phobias regarding flying or living in a skyscraper, but being a lizard I'm more comfortable on a ground floor."

"Perfect, I have just the right place for you," the professor added, as he turned around to face the bookcase behind him. He pulled out a leather bound book which turned out to be hollow. He placed it on his desk and opened it pulling out several small green envelopes from within. He was looking for a specific one and when he found it, he handed it to Sulana.

The envelope read; *"2359 Elmaru Rd."*

"The house key and all the security codes and passwords for access to the net and to me personally, are in there. As soon as I find all the material I have on my book trilogy, I will send it to you. It will probably be a day or so before I can do that," he added. "When you contact me, remember that you can only reach me via audio, although I'll be able to see you through my interface, should you need to show me any reading material or images of any kind."

The professor closed the fake book and put it back on the shelf and as he did, Sulana immediately identified the light footsteps of his Tarsian assistant approaching the office.

Sulana stood up, anticipating that Thula was about to escort her to the roof of the building.

The professor turned around as his assistant opened the door. He smiled at Sulana, and then at Thula, understanding that Sulana's Gulax ears had heard the girl way before his human ears could.

"Well Sulana, I'm glad that you're going to stay with us for a while," he said, extending his hand to say goodbye. "Thula will give you Waldo's and her own private com codes, and I've instructed them to make sure that you don't lack for anything during your stay."

Sulana put her gloves back on and shook the professor's hand. "Thank you, I will wait for your source material with anticipation."

"You'll soon have them in your hands. Goodbye Sulana," the professor said, waving goodbye.

Sulana turned and followed the skinny Tarsian girl through the hallway. As they neared the door leading to the reception area where she had waited to be brought to the professor's office earlier, Thula instead, turned to the right and led her through another much narrower corridor which brought them to an elevator door. The door slid open and the girl gestured for her to enter first. Thula's attitude had definitely changed from their first encounter. Now, she seemed very sweet and eager to please. As the elevator began climbing floors, she brought out a com pad from her tunic and addressed Sulana.

"I need to know your dietary needs so that we can stock the kitchen with the proper foods before you arrive," she stated with a smile.

"Any Terran style leafy greens and vegetables as well as fruits are acceptable. I also like nuts too. For flesh, I prefer rodents such as rats, squirrels, ground hogs and prairie dogs, although I suppose that you don't have any such animals here in Centralia since this planet was terraformed, and therefore, has no native species."

"You are correct Ms. Kay," the Tarsian girl answered. "But we do have chickens, which I understand your species likes as well. And from my planet we have available a six-legged tree dweller that I understand tastes very similar to Terran rodents."

"Thank you. Oh, and so that you understand, I don't eat my prey live like Gulax from The Kural or Gulax Prime do. I was raised on Earth, and we Terran lizards like our flesh freshly butchered cleaned and refrigerated."

Thula nodded and entered the information on her com pad. The elevator reached the roof level and the door opened to a waiting room which led to a private landing pad. The roof had a large skylight through which Sulana could see several fliers high above, traveling in many directions.

"Professor Artemus' flier should be here in a few minutes. Please sit down if you want, and I will wait here with you."

Sulana sat on one of the comfortable couches in the small room, zipped up her jacket and then crossed her arms to remain warm. The waiting room felt like a refrigerator to her. She hoped that her new accommodations could be kept at a decent lizard-like temperature.

Sulana and the Tarsian looked at each other politely a couple of times but remained silent as they waited for the professor's flier. Through her peripheral vision, she caught the girl stealing glances at her on and off. The Tarsian seemed to be fascinated with her.

After a few minutes, the noise of descending thrusters coming from above the landing pad, grew louder in intensity and a large silver and metallic-blue luxury flier plopped softly on the landing pad, its shiny hull gleaming brightly in the late afternoon sun of Centralia.

A set of steps unfolded from its side with a hiss, and out came a tall young pilot wearing a very neat double-breasted black uniform festooned with brass buttons and riding boots. The young man wore white gloves and an old-fashioned military cap.

As the young pilot approached the door to the waiting room, Sulana noticed that he was more of a teenager. He couldn't have been more than sixteen years old. Apparently in Centralia, children were allowed to fly expensive aircraft. He entered the room, removed his cap, showing a tussle of blonde hair and saluted by bowing slightly. His blue eyes reminded her of professor Artemus' eyes.

"Ms. Kay my name is Waldo," he said politely in a very young sounding voice. "I'm ready to take you to your hotel and then to your new residence. Do you have any luggage with you at this time?"

Sulana stood up and thanked Thula for waiting with her. The girl thanked her and said goodbye politely and disappeared into the elevator. "No thank you Waldo. All I have with me is this small briefcase," Sulana answered, pointing to the briefcase.

"May I carry that for you?" he asked, very respectfully.

"It's alright Waldo, I can manage."

Waldo opened the door leading to the landing pad and Sulana stepped into the cold air of the late afternoon. She walked quickly and entered the craft and was relieved to find that the inside was warm and cozy.

Waldo followed her in and closed the door behind him.

The cabin had four very comfortable chairs luxuriously appointed with fine fabrics. Each passenger could look out through their own lightly tinted window next to their seats. Sulana sat on the one furthest from the door.

"Please make sure to adjust your safety belt Ms. Kay, we'll be lifting off in a couple of minutes. Would you like a beverage before we depart?" asked the young man.

"No Waldo, I'm just fine," Sulana answered, trying not to stare too intently at his baby face.

The young man bowed politely one more time and went into the pilot's compartment closing the door behind him. After a minute or so, the hum of the engines grew in intensity and the craft rose smoothly above the university's campus, then it veered east and headed toward the city.

The boy certainly seemed to know how to fly the craft. But he seemed so young! Sulana leaned back on the seat and tried to relax and not be concerned with his age. She remembered that young Kelem Rogeston acquired his Martian Class A pilot's license when he was merely twelve years old. But remembering that fact didn't lessen her apprehension regarding this pilot's abilities. On the other hand, she was sure that Zephron Artemus, who seemed to have immense wealth, would certainly not risk his life daily letting some inexperienced child pilot fly him around if he wasn't confident in the boy's skill.

The flier leveled at about five hundred meters height and picked up speed. The Centralian sun was now dipping below the horizon and darkness was beginning to take over the landscape. Below, Sulana could see the lights of the suburbs glittering here and there. Directly below, the headlights of many land vehicles dotted the many highways leading to and from the city.

"Ms. Kay," came Waldo's voice from inside the pilot's cabin, "I understand that you've been staying at the National Hotel."

"Yes, that's right," Sulana answered, supposing that there was a microphone somewhere in the passenger's cabin.

"May I ask what floor your room is in?" the young pilot asked.

"I'm on the ground floor right in front of the main courtyard. Why do you ask?"

"There are two landing pads at the National. One on the roof of the hotel and the other one behind the courtyard near the land vehicle parking lot. Now I know where to land for your convenience."

"Thank you, Waldo, that's very considerate of you."

"No problem. We'll be landing in about five minutes."

They were now entering Landana proper, the huge capital of Centralia. The flier began climbing higher and leveled at two thousand meters in order to fly above the thousands of kilometer high skyscrapers nestled next to one another as far as the eye could see.

Once a barren planet with no organic life on it, Centralia was chosen to be the center of business and management of the ever-expanding consortium of sovereign planets and solar systems. The Galactic Council chose the planet for its convenient location in the middle of the cluster of civilizations that surrounded it. It took one hundred and fifty years of terraforming and quadrillions of galactic credits, but eventually the planet was made habitable by oxygen breathing species. Within fifty years, it had become the monolithic center of galactic government that it was today.

Below, was a dizzying array of mega structures of every conceivable shape and style. Every major financial institution in the galaxy was headquartered here, as well industrial corporations and a myriad other businesses and organizations involved in the everyday management of over one hundred and fifty civilized species.

The flier slowed down and came to a hover directly above the National Hotel and hung suspended there, waiting for permission to land.

"Ms. Kay," said Waldo through the intercom. "We're about to drop pretty fast down to the landing pad, so please hold on."

Sulana instinctively held her breath and grabbed the arm rests on her chair as the flier suddenly plunged straight down into the National Hotel's lower landing pad.

The main thrusters kicked in and Sulana was temporarily three times heavier than normal as the craft slowed its descent a few meters away from the ground. Seconds later, the craft touched lightly on the landing pad. She had flown thousands of time on fliers much like this one and she had to admit that young Waldo was a top notch pilot after all.

As the engines were winding down, Waldo came out of the pilot's cabin looking sharp as ever and opened the main door. "Ms. Kay unfortunately we're about thirty meters from the rear entrance to the hotel and I'm afraid that you'll have to brave the cold temperature as you make your way to the building."

Sulana zipped up her jacket, climbed down from the flier and walked quickly into the hotel lobby followed by Waldo. A few heads turned around and gawked at the unusual sight of a Gulax. The two of them went straight to her room and once there, she packed her few possessions. When she went to the hotel desk to pay her bill, she was informed that all room charges had been paid in full, courtesy of the management.

She looked up at Waldo and asked, "Is this Professor Artemus' doing?"

"Probably," he replied, nodding his head. "Professor Artemus has many friends in Centralia."

"Curioser and curioser," muttered Sulana under her breath, as she and Waldo walked back to the flier. The good Doctor Zephron Artemus was sure full of surprises. Despite his fame and success as a scholar, his wealth and influence could not possibly be due to book sales alone, though numerous they might be! To Sulana's keen eye and perceptive intellect, Zephron Artemus seemed more like the privileged heir of an old aristocratic family that had enjoyed wealth and position for many generations.

His rags to riches biography also didn't jive in her mind now that she had met the man. Sulana knew that New Lavonia was a backwater planet with little or no resources for it's mainly lower-class mining population. And the local universities and colleges produced nothing but average mining engineers and technicians.

How twelve-year-old Zephron Artemus managed to publish his first book, which became a best seller among scholars and educational institutions across the galaxy from a fringe planet like New Lavonia, was beyond her comprehension. Everything about the man seemed strange and unusual. In particular, his physical appearance! Her quest for the answer to the Rogeston clan's whereabouts had been joined by a new and equally enticing mystery.

Now strapped to her seat on the luxurious flier en route to her new quarters, she wondered if the professor's kindness and generosity could possibly have a hidden purpose. But if there was, what could it possibly be? Was she in any danger? She asked herself. Was she being taken to a gilded cage somewhere in a remote area of the planet?

Her answer came soon after, as Waldo announced through the intercom that they were about to land at the place where she would be staying. As they descended, she saw a large house beneath them, located near the shore of the main artificial sea that had been created in Centralia for its population. Two others existed on the other side of the planet, but this one was the biggest, encompassing several thousand square kilometers.

This time, the flier glided down gently on the landing pad of the house. As soon as the craft touched down, the exterior lights in the garden came to life and the house lights followed suit.

The house was beautiful by any standard. The architecture was both familiar and alien at the same time. The two story structure was surrounded by a beautiful array of trees, plants and bushes that gave the edifice an enchanted cottage quality. The east part of the house faced the sea. Sulana noticed that a two-lane road ran behind the house, and Waldo informed her that the road led to downtown Elmaru, the nearest village which lay about a kilometer away. There was a two seater electric buggy in the garage that she could use to go down to the village or to explore the area if she wished.

When they reached the main entrance, Waldo stood next to her and looked at her expectantly as he held her luggage in his hands. She quickly realized that she needed to find the small envelope that the professor had given her earlier containing the key to the house.

She reached into her briefcase, opened the envelope and took out a key shaped like an electronic chip. She waved it by a metallic plate on the left side of the door's frame and the double door opened inwards revealing a large foyer. A wave of warm air hit her nostrils as she and Waldo entered the house.

"There are two master bedrooms in the house, one downstairs and one upstairs. Which one would you like?" asked Waldo.

"I think the one downstairs," answered Sulana, basking in the soothing warmth of the house.

Waldo walked past the living room and placed her luggage in the downstairs master bedroom on the north side of the house. When he came back, he found Sulana walking through the first floor, getting to know the layout of the house. The living room faced the ocean, and through the large windows, Sulana could see other houses next to this one as the shore curved gently northwards following the edge of the sea. Some of the neighbors, mostly human and apparently unaware of the temperature outside, were sitting on their verandas and terraces enjoying the view and the sound of the waves gently lapping on the beach.

Sulana shivered in disbelief. "Warm blooded species!" she complained, wishing her body could withstand the cold.

"Would you like to see the refrigerator Ms. Kay? I want to make sure that the caretaker stocked it with the right foods," asked Waldo, gesturing toward the kitchen.

Sulana followed him, and upon inspecting the refrigerator, signaled her approval.

When they came back to the stair landing by the door leading to the foyer, Waldo looked back toward the rear of the house and added, "your bedroom is the second one on the right and it has its own private bathroom for your convenience." He put his cap back on his blonde head and stepped closer to the foyer. "If there's nothing else you need Ms. Kay, I'll be taking my leave," he announced, bowing slightly in her direction.

"What about the environmental controls? Are they voice operated?" asked Sulana, concerned about staying warm.

"Yes, Ms. Kay. Temperature and lights respond to standard Galactic commands. Kitchen and bathroom appliances are all manual though." He paused and then asked, "will there be anything else?"

"No thank you Waldo, you've been very accommodating."

"By the way Ms. Kay," Waldo added, "I neglected to give you my card with all my contact information," he added, as he procured a small business card from his left front pocket. "Just so you know, I'll be your personal pilot for the duration. Professor Artemus has freed me of all my regular duties and I am at your disposal whenever you need me, even if it's in the middle of the night. I can be here at the house within a half an hour to pick you up."

"That's very kind of you Waldo, but Thula had already given me all your contact info and I doubt that I'll be asking for your services at three am in the morning!

"In that case I'll be leaving, and please remember that I'm at your disposal anytime!"

He bowed and waved goodbye as he walked out the door.

Waldo closed the front door behind him. She suddenly realized that she hadn't eaten anything since early in the morning and headed to the kitchen to prepare some food. As she opened the refrigerator, the house vibrated slightly as the flier revved up its engines and began to lift off. After a few seconds all was quiet again.

She chopped a few vegetables and made herself a salad. Sitting there eating in the kitchen, she looked through the entrance to the living room at the sea beyond the windows. Centralia had no moon but the immense amount of stars and planets in this part of the galaxy was such that it illuminated the night sky sufficiently to see the movement of waves on the shore. Although she wasn't fond of large bodies of water like most lizards, the gentle swoosh of water calmed her mind.

This house felt safe and comfortable. In some strange way, it felt like a Gulax den. She wondered what was it that gave her that impression, and then she noticed the color scheme of the décor. It was all browns and dark greens and the doors were rounded at the top. The ceilings too were curved. Now that she thought about it, the outside of this house reminded her very much of her parent's house in Johannesburg!

It was almost too perfect she thought. Then she remembered Professor Artemus's words back at his office when he asked if she preferred a top floor or a ground floor, "Perfect, I have just the right place for you," he had said.

Sulana finished her salad, cleaned up the kitchen counter and put the dirty bowl and utensils in the dish washer. She walked into the living room and sat on the biggest couch in the center of the room. She let out a sigh of relief and closed her eyes. She suddenly realized how tired she was, and taking her boots off, she lay down on the couch lengthwise and stretched her long thin frame. Looking up at the room's cathedral ceiling, she listened to all the little noises and creaks of the building. Her sensitive hearing picked up the almost imperceptible hums, clicks and whirrs generated by all the technology in the house.

Most humans would be unaware of the barely audible symphony of activity that was so present in her ears. She focused her hearing on the sound of the gentle waves lapping the edge of the beach outside the house. The couch seemed to mold to the shape of her body and she felt very warm and comfortable. Before she knew it she was fast asleep.

CHAPTER 2

Thula's Visit

Agong was ringing somewhere in the distance. In her dream she was a child again and the school bell was calling the children back to class.

The ringing was persistent, and she began to get angry at the repeating clanging in her ears. She sat up with a start ready to yell at whoever it was that kept playing that gong so loud, only to remember where she was. She turned her eyes toward the windows facing the sea and the bright light of the Centralian sun made her secondary eyelids close instinctively. The ringing, she realized, was the front doorbell.

She stood up to go to answer the door and noticed that she had taken off her tunic sometime during the night.

Lizards have no cultural taboos regarding nakedness, but she knew other species did. She slipped her tunic back on and went to answer the door.

When she opened the foyer door, she saw Thula's face on the door's digi-screen. She wondered how the Tarsian girl had gotten to the house. The noise of a lander would have surely awakened her. Still, she could have been so deeply asleep that she hadn't heard the noise of the craft's engines.

She opened the door and shivered as a blast of cool morning air blew into the house from the garden. "Good morning Ms. Kay, may come in?" Thula greeted her with a cheerful smile.

"Of course," answered Sulana, letting her in then quickly closing the door. She looked at the landing pad in the garden and noticed that there was no flyer parked outside.

This morning the Tarsian girl was wearing a traditional Tarsian dress full of intricate embroideries, depicting scenes of plant and animal life on Tarsia Prime. The dress complemented her thin frame.

"I'm sorry to disturb you so early in the morning, but I found all of professor Artemus' research material on the Rogeston Trilogy, and he asked me to bring it to you personally rather than send it to you through the net."

"Really?" Sulana replied, her brain just beginning to wake up. "You can thank the professor for his kind gesture, but I would have been satisfied to receive the materials digitally."

"The professor is very security conscious, and even though the Rogeston books have been published, he felt that it would be safer for me to bring you his research in person should you discover a fact that he somehow missed in the past."

"I understand his concern," Sulana commented, while gesturing to Thula to enter the living room. Perhaps the good professor is worried that his reputation could be diminished should someone else discover that he missed something, Sulana thought to herself.

"He would immediately contact his publishers and inform them of any corrections that needed to be included in any future printing of the books," the Tarsian girl added as she sat on the couch opposite the one Sulana had spent the night in. The girl's comment made Sulana feel as if the Tarsian had read her mind. "And of course, you would get credit for any new information your own research brings to light," she concluded.

"That is most gracious of him," Sulana added, as she reached down for her boots on the floor and slipped them on. "But if I find what I'm looking for and my theories regarding the fate of the Rogeston clan prove right, my efforts will definitely affect the professor's current versions of the books on the family."

Thula looked down and a hint of a smile flashed on her face for an instant, but quickly disappeared. Sulana caught the gesture on the young girl's face with her lizard's peripheral vision and wondered what it meant.

"May I offer you something to drink? Perhaps a tea?" offered Sulana, acting as if she hadn't seen the girl's subtle reaction to her statement.

"Oh yes. A hot tea would be nice. It's kind of chilly outside."

Sulana walked to the kitchen and found a tea kettle and a variety of exotic tea blends from all over the galaxy in the pantry.

"What's your preference?" Sulana asked, from the kitchen.

"Any green tea will do," came the response from the living room.

As she was pouring the hot water in the teacups, Thula walked to the kitchen. She stopped by the door and leaned on the door frame watching Sulana pour the hot water. "What do you think happened to the Rogestons?" she asked casually.

Sulana knew that the Tarsian, being the professor's assistant, had been privy to all the communiqués between Zephron Artemus and herself. She was surely aware of Sulana's quest for the fate of the Rogestons. But the girl was probing Sulana's mind for something other than the obvious answer to her query.

"I think they're still around," Sulana said quietly, while stirring the tea. "I want to find them and ask them several questions."

"What would you ask them?"

"I want to know where they all are, or at least where they went after 2965. I'm sure their descendants know exactly what happened after the family left Plantanimus. I also suspect that Kelem, Anima and many of the others are still alive somehow."

"But Ms. Kay that's impossible! All the Plantanimals died when the Dreamers perished. Everyone knows that," Thula countered, her tone revealing her opinion.

"I don't agree. I think that Tatiana Rogeston created new bodies for all the family. Even the Plantanimal Rogestons."

"All the bodies that Tatiana's method helped create did prolong life but for only a few decades. And the younger Rogeston descendants still in human form at the time of the Dreamers demise, told everyone that Tatiana's method did not work on Plantanimal bodies due to the nature of the very matter that their bodies were made of. What makes you think they lied?" the girl argued.

Sulana decided to open up to the Tarsian girl and confess a few facts that she hadn't admitted to anyone since she began her research. She would have to tell Zephron Artemus eventually anyway.

"I'm going to tell you something that I haven't told anyone, not even professor Artemus."

Thula stopped leaning on the door frame, walked over to the kitchen counter and faced Sulana, her eyes full of curiosity.

After a few moments' hesitation, Sulana began talking in a conspiratorial tone. "I went to Plantanimus last year on the pretext that I was a vacationing student. After running into so many dead ends in my research, I decided to take matters into my own hands, sort to speak." Sulana paused, looking at her reptilian hands and then left and right as if others might be listening to her conversation just outside the kitchen.

Leaning slightly forward, Thula's upwardly slanted eyes and eyebrows rose in anticipation of what the Gulax would say next.

"I didn't go alone. I was accompanied by a Tarsian anthropologist by the name of Dr. Rimun Gurwat and a Terran forensics expert named Louis Marchant. I met the anthropologist in the course of my research and found out that he also had serious questions about the Rogeston's ultimate fate. It turned out that he'd been investigating the history of the Rogestons for many years and our theories and conjectures were very similar."

"And the Terran, what about him?" asked the girl, with great interest.

"He heard of our plan to go to Plantanimus through a friend of Dr. Gurwat and approached us asking if he could join the expedition. He claimed his ancestors were related to the Rogestons by marriage going back to the 22nd century, and that his hobby had been about all things Rogeston since his teenage years. Both claims proved to be right. His collection of Rogeston memorabilia and personal items were almost as impressive as Dr. Gurwat's. At first, I was reticent to include him in our plan, but when I found out that he was a well-respected forensics expert in the Terran Solar System, I welcomed him, realizing that his expertise could prove useful."

Thula tilted her head questioningly. "How so?"

"Well, I timed our arrival to Plantanimus on the last week of the tourist season. We stayed well beyond the closing of the park and procured lodging at the only hotel that stays open all through the Plantanimal year at the mouth of the river delta near the old Rogeston compound. From then until the end of the winter solstice, the planet is manned only by a small contingent of park rangers. That particular year, we were lucky in that we were the only tourists left on the entire planet for the winter season. Our cover was that we were members of an extreme fundamentalist branch of the Church of St. Kelem and that we'd come to pray and meditate on Mount Olympus at the feet of the old Dreamers."

"Did your cover work?" asked Thula, captivated by Sulana's tale.

"Yes!" exclaimed Sulana, uncharacteristically excited for a Gulax. "No one bothered us the entire time we stayed on Plantanimus. The few Rangers left on duty soon got used to seeing us running around the place and eventually left us alone for weeks on end." Sulana picked up her cup and motioned to Thula do the same and join her in the living room. The two females walked to the living room and sat on separate couches facing each other.

They each took a few sips of tea in silence and eventually put their cups down on the coffee table. Thula crossed her arms and leaned forward waiting to hear more.

"Louis Marchant, the forensics expert, had managed to borrow a flyer from a wealthy relative of his and brought it with us on the transport that took us to Plantanimus. We had full run of the entire planet. In the flyer's cargo hold he'd stashed a great complement of forensic equipment which is what we used to discover some very interesting facts."

"What did you discover?" queried Thula, now thoroughly enthralled by the story.

"We sneaked into the old Rogeston House one night and managed to recover DNA material from hairs that fortunately were still caught in the drains in the five bathrooms of the house. Luckily, most of the samples were in perfect condition, despite the passage of time. Marchant examined the DNA and compared it to hair samples that we took from a hairbrush on display at Kelem and Anima's cottage by the waterfall at the edge of the Dreamer forest. He was sure that the white hairs on the brush were Kelem's while still in human form. We also had Kelem's DNA pattern from his medical records on Mars. And indeed, the white hair samples from the brush turned out to be his. But when we compared Kelem's DNA samples with those from the house, we discovered that there were no familial markers between the two groupings."

"Really? None?" asked Thula, seemingly shocked by the news.

"That's right. None. We continued analyzing the rest of the samples and managed to distinguish twelve separate individual patterns from the house. There was one human Caucasian male sample which we discovered was Alexei's, and one mostly Tarsian female sample with a strange, but small mutation, which appeared to be of human origin. We were sure this was Kani's and then, ten Human/Tarsian hybrid samples which were surely their children's DNA."

"So, are you saying that Alexei and Kani Rogeston and their children were not blood relatives of Kelem Rogeston?"

"Apparently not," retorted Sulana, sounding troubled. "You are the first person to know of these discoveries beside myself, Dr. Gurwat and Louis Marchant. Think of it! For hundreds of years, everyone assumed that Alexei was a direct descendant of Kelem. It appears that the family which we've regarded as Rogestons for so long, is not related to Kelem at all! What's frustrating, is that the public can't know of this, since all this data was acquired illegally, much less be included in my dissertation."

"You can rely on me to maintain secrecy. But you must tell professor Artemus of your findings." Thula advised, sounding concerned.

"I intend to tell him about the DNA controversy as well as the rest."

"You mean there's more?" Thula questioned, this time sounding really surprised.

"Well, for one thing, the Rogeston cemetery near the old compound is totally fake. Except for two bodies, whose gravestones were inscribed with Alexei and Kani's names. The rest of the two hundred some odd graves in the cemetery were empty. We tested the ground on each and every empty grave and didn't find a single DNA strand belonging to any Rogeston family member."

"You didn't..." uttered Thula in disbelief... fearing Sulana and her cohorts had desecrated the Alexei and Kani's graves.

"No of course not!" Replied Sulana, slightly offended by Thula's suspicion that she, Dr. Gurwat and Louis Marchant had disinterred the two bodies from their resting place. "We used ground penetrating radar on those two graves and nothing else. We found that one body was definitely a male human and the other one a female Tarsian. Both sets of bones matched the measurements of Alexei and Kani as recorded in human and Tarsian historical documents." Sulana's voice trailed off as she leaned back on the couch and sighed. She looked out and noticed the sun's shadows shortening below the garden plants as it climbed in the sky. "Whoever they were, they were surely quite old by the time they were interred. Through the radar image, we could tell that the decalcification in their bones was quite advanced. Louis figured that they must have been around one hundred and thirty, or perhaps one hundred and forty by the time they died."

While Sulana's gaze was directed toward the garden, the Tarsian girl's eyes betrayed a certain sadness which she managed to hide by the time the Gulax turned her head back toward her.

Composing herself, she asked casually, "do you believe that the remains belonged to Alexei and Kani Rogeston?"

"Of all the unanswered mysteries regarding the Rogestons, I believe that those two graves most likely belonged to Alexei and Kani. I felt honored to stand at the foot of the graves of the progenitors of the first generation of Rogeston children on Plantanimus, regardless of their bloodline."

"What convinced you that those two graves were Alexei's and Kani's?"

"There is a chapter near the end of professor Artemus' "Biography of Kelem Rogeston" in which he quotes from an interview of Kelem by a Terran reporter circa 2865. It was one of the few times Kelem Rogeston ever spoke to anyone in the media, particularly after becoming a Plantanimal. By then, the secret of Plantanimus had been discovered several years prior to this interview and the blockade of the planet was but a few years in the future. Professor Artemus' opinion is that Rogeston himself arranged for the interview with the reporter in an effort to educate the public at large regarding the true nature of the Dreamers, Plantanimals and the members of the Rogeston family. In it he described a conversation that he had with his youngest granddaughter Tatiana who was seventeen at the time just before she traveled to Earth for the first time. However, when this interview took place, Tatiana was already one hundred years old and would soon return to Plantanimus to help manage the military blockade."

"Most of the subject matter relating to this portion of his conversation with young Tatiana dealt with the nature of life, death and rebirth as a Plantanimal. At one point, he tells his granddaughter that some people like her mother and father, might choose not to prolong their lives by transitioning into Plantanimal bodies. The girl is apparently surprised to hear this and he forewarns her not to be disappointed."

Thula sat quietly, her eyes fixed on the wood grain of the coffee table as Sulana paused to sip some more tea. Her eyes shifted beyond Sulana's figure looking at the garden through the window behind Sulana's couch. A breeze came by and rattled the leaves of a Japanese maple tree in the garden. She closed her eyes and raised her chin slightly, as if remembering or visualizing something in her mind.

Sulana noticed the girl's closed eyes and thought perhaps she'd gotten bored with the explanation of her conclusions. But immediately Thula opened her eyes and eagerly asked her to continue.

"Rogeston goes on to tell the reporter that Tatiana's parents had indeed decided not to extend their normal life span," continued Sulana. "And Professor Artemus concludes that Alexei and Kani died sometime during the planet's thirty-six-year blockade. His conclusion coincides with my findings."

"So you agree with the professor's conclusion?"

"Absolutely. When I read that part of the book, something in me told me that it was true. I honestly believe that Alexei and Kani are the two people in those graves. However, don't ask me to corroborate my findings," Sulana stated, almost defensively. "I have many, many loose ends in my mind regarding my conclusions and hunches about the Rogeston family."

Thula's face softened and a look of compassion and tenderness showed in her eyes. "You are troubled by these feelings and unsubstantiated conclusions of yours?"

"Yes!" exhaled Sulana, as she leaned back on the couch, seemingly exhausted by the telling of her tale. "I've already confessed my un-Gulax like obsession with the Rogestons to the professor. And even though he's shown me such kindness and support in my quest, I'm sure that he thinks that I'm on a fool's errand." Sulana said, then reached for her cup, finished her tea, stood up and walked over to the windows facing the beach. "Perhaps he's right," she said softly, almost to herself.

Thula stood up and walked over to the window next to Sulana. She looked out to the sea as well and after a short while she spoke. "Don't be too quick to think that professor Artemus doubts your theories or the importance of your research. It's obvious to me that you've uncovered significant discrepancies regarding the historical record of the Rogeston family. I think that when he hears all that you just told me, he'll want you to continue with your research."

Sulana's mood was raised by the young girl's positive words. She turned and looked at the professor's young assistant with new eyes and came to the realization that perhaps she'd been too quick to judge the Tarsian, based on her behavior in the first few minutes of their acquaintance.

"Do you really think so?" Sulana asked, hoping that Thula's belief in the good professor's support was accurate.

"I know the man well and I understand how he thinks," Thula answered. Then, she walked over to Sulana and reached for her hand.

Sulana almost shrunk at the gesture. Like Tarsians, Gulax don't like to be touched and she knew that even humans accustomed to living and working with lizards did not enjoy the feel and touch of a Gulax's cold leathery skin and carefully avoided the sharpness of their yellowish claws. Sulana always wore gloves when in mixed company for that reason.

Thula took Sulana's bare hand without hesitation. The warmth of her human flesh felt good touching hers. Sulana relaxed and suddenly felt as if a heavy weight had been lifted from her shoulders, and at the same time, she experienced a strange sense of elation that she couldn't help but be surprised at. Lizards keep their emotions buried deep within their psyche, and this sudden rush of lightheartedness was very unusual in her.

Thula smiled brightly, her green eyes sparkling in the light coming from the window. She looked deep into Sulana's eyes and spoke in a gentle voice. "There's an old quote from one of Shakespeare's plays that says;" "Who could refrain that had a heart to love and in that heart courage to make love known?"

The quote made Sulana think that she had heard these words before, but the feeling was more like a hint of a long lost memory or a dream that she'd once had a long time ago. Shakespeare's words seemingly had nothing to do with her frustration from the struggle to find the answer to the Rogestons' fate. Yet, they made her feel that she would eventually find the answer to her questions.

"I don't quite know why you mentioned that quote to me right now, but it made me feel better about things," Sulana said, looking down at her hand still being held by Thula's.

"You looked like you needed to hear something pleasant to sooth your troubled soul," Thula said softly, while letting go of her hand.

Now separated, both turned their eyes back to the sea. Even though they were no longer holding hands, Sulana still felt connected to the Tarsian girl in some ineffable way.

Thula turned to Sulana again. "I have to go back to the university now, but I'll be free in the evening if you'd like to talk to me or wish me to come by and visit you again."

"I would like that very much Thula. I usually like to spend time by myself. But somehow, being on this planet has made me feel the need for the company of others."

"Perhaps you'd like to come to our house tonight and spend some time with me and my friends," Thula offered, then paused to explain. "You see, I live with a few close friends that I've known for a long time and we all share in the running of the house. We're more like a family than anything else, and I think that you'd enjoy meeting them."

"That sounds very nice. Can I let you know later if I can come tonight? Sulana countered, trying not to sound too eager to be in the company of Thula's friends. "I might get caught up in my research, and once I get involved it's hard for me to stop."

"I understand. Just let me know through the net or call me directly."

"I will," Sulana added, going back to the coffee table and picking up the empty teacups. She went to the kitchen and placed the cups in the dishwasher.

Thula followed her to the kitchen and presented her with a memory chip. "This is the professor's material on the trilogy. It's a copy of the original, but please, guard it as if it were the original."

"Absolutely," she agreed, putting the chip in her tunic's pocket. "And would you please also thank the professor for me? It seems that he paid for my hotel bill in full. Tell him that I am eternally grateful to him for that. I've spent nearly all my savings chasing the Rogestons and after this trip to Centralia I was going to have to go back to Earth and find some kind of employment in order to continue my research."

"I will pass on your message of appreciation to him. And please, don't worry about the length of your stay here with us on Centralia. As you well know, the professor is quite wealthy and he has offered his generous hospitality to many other seekers of truth in the past. You are definitely a welcomed guest."

"I suppose you can call my research a kind of 'pursuit of the truth', but you can assure him that I will not overstay my welcome if I don't find anything significant in his Trilogy notes."

"Of course. Meanwhile, if you need anything, remember that Waldo is at your beckoned call. The house's main com panel is in the studio at the other end of the house," Thula informed her, pointing west to the rear of the house facing the road.

Sulana was about to thank Thula for her visit when the roar of a flyer's retros rattled the windows in the house.

"That's for me," Thula said, pointing to the garden.

Sulana turned and looked through the house's south windows just in time to catch a beautiful Tarsian flyer come to a gentle stop on the garden's landing pad. The ship's iridescent green hull glistened brightly in the morning sunlight. This was no common utility flyer. Sulana knew a thing or two about Tarsian technology, and this vessel was one of the most advanced ones that she had ever seen. She turned and looked at Thula with an impressed look.

"That's my brother Vardik's flyer," Thula mentioned casually. "We both work for the professor."

"I see," responded Sulana, somewhat at a loss for words.

The flyer's door opened and a young distinguished looking Tarsian male wearing a traditional tunic, stepped down and walked toward the house.

By the time Sulana and Thula had reached the foyer and opened the door, Vardik was already standing there. He bowed politely and greeted Sulana in Gulaxian.

"Tas dreek umtar," (Good morning)

"Good morning to you, Vardik," responded Sulana, somewhat tentatively. She felt a bit embarrassed that she knew very little Gulaxian, having been raised on Terra. Her parents spoke Gulaxian but hardly ever used it.

"Good morning brother, this is Ms. Sulana Kay, Professor Artemus' house guest."

"Ah, yes. I knew you were staying here. It's a pleasure to meet you Ms. Kay. Welcome to Centralia," he added, in standard galactic.

"Thank you Vardik. Would you like to come in?" she asked.

"Unfortunately, not at this time Ms. Kay. I must deliver my sister to the professor's office by one dash ten am. But I hope to meet you again soon."

"I've invited Sulana to come to our house perhaps this evening if she's available." Thula mentioned, looking expectantly at Sulana.

"Yes, perhaps we'll see each other this evening," responded Sulana, still trying to sound undecided.

"Fine perhaps this evening then," Vardik added with a smile, and then turned to Thula. "Are your ready sister?

"Yes, I am." Thula grabbed Sulana, then gave her a gentle hug and whispered in her ear. "I hope you'll come tonight."

Vardik bowed once again and headed for the landing pad. Thula waved goodbye and followed her brother.

Sulana went back inside the house and watched intently as the beautiful Tarsian flyer pushed against the gravity of Centralia and climbed higher and higher, until it blended with the rest of the air traffic high above the suburbs.

As she stood there while still looking at the sky through the window, it suddenly dawned on her that so far, everyone involved with professor Zephron Artemus was unusual in one way or another.

"What an unusual group of people." Sulana thought, as she walked back to the living room. "To begin with, there's the professor, a famous and unusually wealthy superstar of academia, who looks half his chronological age and keeps that fact zealously hidden from the public at large. Add to that, someone who's had his head wired for wireless communication, and whose office is crammed with priceless antiques. Then, there's his incredibly young staff, one of whom is apparently wealthy beyond measure as well, and the other a barely pubescent-boy-pilot who flies like nobody's business. And then, Thula's brother Vardik who carries himself like Tarsian royalty just like his sister."

Back in the living room, she lay back on the couch staring at the ceiling deep in thought. "And then there's me!" she added wistfully, "an obsessive-compulsive law-breaking lizard with a penchant for solving a mystery that no one in the galaxy seems to give a damn about!

And here she was, staying in a luxurious house owned by the famous professor (one of many she was sure), who had previously stated that although he didn't think that she would find anything of value in his original research, had nevertheless rolled out the red carpet for her and had given her carte blanche for an unlimited amount of time.

None of it made sense. Yet, she was following this strange path that had been laid for her by circumstances. Being a lizard, she was hardly susceptible to idealizing or romanticizing situations as humans and Tarsians were prone to do. She felt as if an unseen hand was guiding her decisions. Merely a participant in a play.

She put her hand in her tunic's pocket and felt the professor's data chip in her fingers. She jumped up from the couch and walked to the back of the house looking for the studio where Thula had said the main com panel would be located.

She found it right away and once inside, gave a verbal command to activate the system. The windows in the room darkened to minimize daylight, and an antique oak desk, very similar to the one the professor had in his office, came to life as a large holographic screen and keyboard materialized out of thin air above its finely polished surface. Sulana shook her head in wonderment. Even in the 33rd century, this technology was cutting edge. She took the data chip out of her tunic and a square portion of the desk with a slot for a chip, rose about ten centimeters to meet her hand.

Sulana laughed softly. "Maybe this thing is so smart it will do the work for me," she commented, amused.

She slipped the chip in, and several folder icons instantly popped up in the virtual screen. They were all dated. The oldest was seventeen years old. Sulana smiled and tried to visualize what the professor must have looked like when he worked on this project. "He was probably little more than a toddler recently toilet trained most likely!" She remarked dryly.

She took a deep breath, sat on the plush leather chair and opened the oldest folder titled, "KR DATA-06/25/3215. Several documents related to Kelem Rogeston appeared on the screen. She zoomed in on his birth certificate and began to work.

Several hours later she took a break and spoke out loud, "house, what time is it?"

"It is eight thirty eight, second daily period," answered the A.I. Time on Centralia was split into three daily periods, Morning, Afternoon and Evening, (1, 2 & 3) each consisting of twelve segments lasting approximately forty Terran minutes per segment. Altogether, the Centralian day lasted exactly twenty-four Terran hours.

Sulana's stomach was growling. She hadn't stopped working on the professor's notes since Thula had left early in the morning. She got up from the chair in the studio and went to the kitchen to prepare some food. This time she wanted some meat. She opened the refrigerator and found a pack named, "Greelk-Tarsian Tree Dweller". She popped the vacuum seal and smelled the raw flesh with her tongue. It was indeed very similar in smell to a Terran rodent. The animal appeared to be about thirty centimeters long including the tail and it had six limbs. It had been butchered very neatly. Its skin, head, claws and innards removed. She put the chicken-like flesh on a plate in the kitchen counter and saw that except for its tail the animal had been expertly de-boned. Sulana cut the tail off, threw it away and then snipped a small piece of the torso with kitchen scissors. She carefully put it in her mouth and nibbled on it for a few seconds trying to decide whether she liked the taste or not. After a short while, she decided that it was acceptable and she consumed most of the meat in a short time. She poured herself some Tarsian fruit juice, then made herself some green tea and went back to the studio to continue with her research

CHAPTER 3

The Mansion in The Ranes Valley

She had been working for several hours and hadn't even gone through one quarter of the original folder that she had opened earlier that morning and there were at least eighty more folders to go through. "This is going to take a lot longer than I thought!" she said to herself at one point.

Much of what was in this first folder was familiar to her, except for some Martian newspaper articles dating back from the years 2601 through 2627. They all dealt mostly mostly with Muir and Jocelyn Rogeston, Kelem's parents as well as two articles about Kelem's adoption by his uncle and aunt Bernardo and Margarita Salas in 2621 when the Martian Family Court granted them permanent custody of then, six year old Kelem.

However, none of what she had read so far added any significant new data to her own research. She felt a little disappointed by this but she was more concerned by her lack of concentration today.

Her mind kept wandering. Her conversation with Thula early that morning kept circling back to her mind. She felt a little unsettled by her experience when the young Tarsian girl had touched her hand. She had never felt a sensation like the one she experienced when Thula's flesh met hers. And afterwards, Sulana kept feeling as if the two of them were still holding hands long after Thula had left for the University with her brother.

Several times today she had looked out to the garden whenever she heard a flyer landing in one of the houses nearby, hoping that it might be Thula coming back. If she were human she might say that she was physically attracted to the Tarsian girl and that she had become infatuated with her. But Sulana knew that it had nothing to do with interspecies romance or sexuality.

No, this was different. She was having a hard time admitting it to herself. The more she avoided it the more her subconscious kept nagging at her. "She, (dare she think it?) felt spiritually connected to Thula."

Most Lizards from Gulaxia conducted their lives by means of logic and common sense. However, Terran lizards had adopted many human mores and ethics through the centuries and in the last few decades, some had involved themselves in religious pursuits. Many Terran religious groups recruited the earlier Gulax immigrants when they came to Earth. Some had even joined the Church of St. Kelem.

An hour later, she found herself unable to think of nothing else. "This is embarrassing!" she chided herself for her lack of concentration. "I'm a graduate student of history with years of research experience. What's wrong with me!"

She threw her arms in the air in frustration and leaned back in the chair closing her eyes. Cradling her hands behind her head she sat there hoping to clear her mind of whatever this thing was, but to no avail.

She looked at the time counter in the computer screen and it read "2-9:30". The second daily period was almost over and the sun's shadows were lengthening in the garden. Soon it would be dark and she found herself wondering when Thula would call to ask if she'd decided to accept her invitation for this evening. She'd had enough of research for one day. She saved her work and was about to shut down the computer when a soft chime rang announcing an incoming call.

"Answer call," she ordered the house.

Thula's beautiful face framed by her long black hair, appeared on the screen.

"Hello Sulana, it's me Thula. Will you allow visual?" she asked.

"Allow visual," Sulana ordered, feeling unusually excited.

"Have you decided to accept our invitation?"

"Yes Thula, I would very much like to come to your house tonight. When do you want me to arrive?"

"Oh, there's no need for you to procure transportation. We live on the other side of Elmaru. We'll come pick you up by land."

Oh, I see," Sulana replied.

"We'll pick you up around "3-2" said Thula." Sulana had to do the math in her head and understood that it would be two and a half hours from now.

"I'll be ready for you."

"By the way, bundle up because it's going to get chilly tonight. We're supposed to have early snow flurries this evening and our buggy is not heated."

"Really?" Sulana responded, worrying about what Thula meant by "chilly".

As if she was reading Sulana's mind she continued. "Don't worry, we're only a few kilometers away and we'll bring some extra blankets to throw on you while we drive back."

"That's most considerate of you. Believe me, you don't want a lethargic lizard on your hands when I meet your friends. By the way, does this 'buggy' have doors and windows?" she asked, as casually as she could.

Thula laughed out loud, her face turning slightly darker green. "Yes, of course it does," Answered Thula smiling. "You'll only be exposed to the elements while getting in and out of the buggy."

"Well that's a relief!"

"Wonderful. We'll see you at "3-2"."

"Three dash two," repeated Sulana.

Thula's face blinked out, and the screen went back to displaying all of professor Artemus' folder icons once again.

Sulana gave the verbal command for the computer to shut off, and left the studio heading for her bedroom. She undressed, went to the bathroom and took a long steam bath followed by a moisturizing spray. The bathroom closet had a rack of nice bathrobes, the kind that lizards like, all made of thick and soft material. Sulana put on the biggest and warmest one and plopped herself on the large supple bed.

The house suddenly spoke. "Ms. Kay, are you about to enter into a slumber period? May I remind you that you have guests arriving at three dash two. Do you want me to set up a wake-up call at three dash one?"

Pleased knowing that the house's A.I. was advanced enough to know that she had company coming, she sat for a minute and decided that a short nap would do her a world of good. "Yes," she responded. "Wake me up at three dash one with a soft gong and not too loud please! I'm a lizard with sensitive ears."

"Yes Ms. Kay I'm aware of your species' requirements," the A.I informed her.

As she laid down wrapped in the soft bathrobe, it only took a few seconds before she was fast asleep.

Sulana dreamt that she was back on Plantanimus walking up the path on Mount Olympus leading to the ancient caldera where Zeus, the eldest Dreamer's body was. When she reached the mouth of the caldera, she heard a strange voice beckoning her to come closer to his trunk. The deep voice sounded vaguely familiar but she couldn't place its owner's identity.

"WELCOME CHILD, LET'S TALK," the voice boomed. Its echo rumbling through the forest's floor as it vibrated through her body."

"What shall I say?" Sulana responded, somewhat intimidated by the voice's powerful effect.

"YOU HAVE MANY QUESTIONS DO YOU NOT?"

She opened her mouth to ask the first question but for some reason she couldn't remember what the question was!

"WELL?" thundered the voice, impatiently.

"I… I can't think of anything!" she shouted back, panicking.

"PERHAPS YOU HAVE NOTHING TO SAY?" the voice said quizzically.

"No, no, wait a minute! I need answers to my questions, but I seem to have forgotten them now!" she shouted in frustration.

"IF YOU HAVE NO QUESTIONS, PERHAPS YOU ALREADY KNOW THE ANSWERS."

"How can I know the answers when I can't remember the questions?" Sulana complained, feeling very upset.

"WRONG QUESTIONS RESULT IN WRONG ANSWERS," the deep voice pronounced ominously. Its booming echoes followed by an eerie silence.

In the silence, Sulana struggled to understand what was happening. She knew something was wrong but couldn't figure out what it was. She ran to the foot of the enormous plant sitting in the middle of the crater and kneeled by it, tears suddenly streaming from her reptilian eyes. Her body shook as she wept in painful desperation, her fists banging on the roots of the Dreamer. Her tears became a flowing river that poured around Zeus's massive body. His trunk shuddered and a low vibration began growing and gaining in intensity until it became an unbearably beautiful symphony of exotic sounds such as she had never heard before. The music's volume rose higher and higher until it sounded like thunder bolts striking her ears. Her body's atomic structure began to vibrate sympathetically with the music until it lost its cohesion. In a blinding flash Sulana's body dissolved into a trillion quantum particles and became a sparkling mist floating above the forest's floor. The mist settled near Zeus's roots and blended itself with his body. She was at once Sulana and Zeus the Dreamer in one body.

A soothing gentle voice spoke in her ears. "Time to wake up Sulana, time to wake up."

Sulana woke up startled and jumped up from the bed so forcefully that she landed on the floor on her knees. Her heart was pounding and she felt disoriented.

"Are you injured Ms. Kay, should I call for medical assistance?" asked the house's A.I.

Sulana raised herself from the floor and sat on the bed, holding her head in her hands. "No, I'm alright there's no emergency."

"Sensors show that your heart rate is unusually fast for your species. Would you like to take a calmant?" The A.I. asked, with a concerned inflection in its voice.

"I'm alright, I just had a weird dream that's all," Sulana answered, as the fog of sleep cleared from her brain.

"It is three dash one past one-minute Ms. Kay. Please remember that you have guests arriving in fifty-nine minutes, Centralian."

"Yes, thank you," responded Sulana, as she made her way to the bathroom. When she stepped in front of the sink to douse some water On her face, she was shocked to see the tracks of tears on her face. Female Gulax typically cry only during childbirth or when mourning the death of a parent or child.

Sulana had never cried in her life. Curious, she flashed her reptile tongue out and physically licked the liquid from her face. Her tears tasted very similar to Human and Tarsian tears a fact that she'd learned in school as a child but had never experienced personally. Once in primary school, one of her human friends had hurt himself on the playground and he began to cry. Sulana helped the little boy get up from the floor and took him to the school nurse. While there she asked him if it was alright to taste his tears and he let her. Now her reaction to crying was both pleasing and alarming at the same time. She sat on the bench next to the steam room door and tried to make sense of what had just happened. With her emotions once again in check, she regained control of herself. She wasn't distraught, but she wasn't calm either. Twice today, she'd had two unusual experiences, both connected to the Rogestons in an oblique way.

In all the years pursuing the mystery of the Rogeston clan, she'd never once dreamed of Zeus or anyone in the family. This dream had been so powerful and different, it had a "you are there" quality to it. An aspect that had not been in Sulana's dreams before. Furthermore, the intense moment when Thula's hand touched hers earlier today, and the residual effect of feeling connected to the Tarsian girl, added to the strangeness of the day.

Sulana recounted the events in her mind since she had arrived in Centralia, and she had to admit that so far, nothing had gone according to plan. Just about everything and everyone that she'd met up to now, had turned out to be unusual and different. For a moment, fear took the best of her and she thought of packing her bags and getting the hell out of this planet to avoid getting entangled in a situation that could get out of control. But beneath the insecurity and paranoia, an unspoken but persistent voice kept telling her to stay and keep following her search.

Feeling strengthened in her resolve, she slapped her hands on her thighs, and began to get ready for tonight's visit to Thula's house. She picked the warmest coveralls that she'd brought with her, a red one that had a hood, in case Thula's house was too cold for a lizard. She hoped that with gloves and a thick jacket, she could stay warm.

At three dash two on the dot, the front doorbell rang and when she went to the foyer, she saw Thula's head on the door screen. She noticed that the girl's head was wrapped in some kind of scarf or hat. This told Sulana that it was surely cold outside. She pulled up the hood on her coveralls, closed her jacket, put on her gloves and braved opening the door.

A blast of cold air hit Sulana's face almost making her gasp.

"Good evening Sulana, let's get you into the buggy!" said Thula hurriedly.

Sulana closed the door, swiped the key past the lock, and holding herself tightly, ran through the garden following Thula to the road behind the house. On the shoulder, sat a four-wheel electric buggy, its silver body gleaming softly in the Centralian night sky.

As they reached the vehicle, the front and rear doors opened. Thula signaled for Sulana to get into the back of the buggy as she entered in the front. Thula was laughing, as she and Sulana slammed the doors simultaneously.

"Brrrr, it's really cold tonight!" she said with excitement in her voice. "It usually doesn't get this cold until later in the year, but people are saying that the planet's weather is changing since it was terraformed."

Sulana, too cold to talk, just nodded her head. When she looked to the driver's side she realized that there was a human male sitting there.

"Oh, I forgot to introduce you to each other" Thula said, pointing to the man sitting at the wheel. "This is Omega Jones, one of my friends."

"Sulana Kay's my name. Pleasure to meet you," muttered Sulana barely able to talk.

"Likewise, I'm sure," responded the middle aged man politely, as he pulled away from the house. The man's deep blue eyes looked at Sulana intently though the rearview mirror. In the semidarkness of the vehicle's interior, Sulana studied the man who appeared to be in his mid-sixties.

She realized that this was the first older person that she had met through professor Artemus. He had short brown hair and appeared to be of European/Caucasian origin, although his accent was not Terran.

"Oh dear," uttered Thula, interrupting Sulana's study of the man at the wheel. "You must be freezing. Here are the blankets I promised you," Thula added, as she handed Sulana a bundle of them.

Sulana quickly wrapped herself in them and began to feel better right away.

As they headed toward Thula's house, the terrain began to climb slightly. Soon, the road veered to the left and all the houses by the sea became smaller and smaller until Sulana could only see their rooftops. They were in open country now and the buggy began to gather speed. The semidarkness of the Centralian night illuminated the short scrubby vegetation passing by in a blur. The plant which was prevalent on the planet was a quick growing variety of dessert bush that the terraforming engineers had found on one of the Tareean worlds. It was one of the main sources of oxygen on Centralia and it was everywhere. After a few more minutes, the ground leveled off and Sulana saw that they had climbed about three hundred meters, and a small but deep valley with dwellings and other types of buildings lay ahead.

"That's Ranes up ahead," said Thula, pointing down as the buggy dipped down into a steep winding dirt road, leading to what appeared to be a small town.

"Did you say Ranes? As in the continent on Plantanimus?" asked Sulana, surprised to hear the name.

"Yes that's right."

"Who named the town?" asked Sulana, her curiosity peaked.

"Oh, it's not a town. It's a private reserve managed by a non-profit organization." Thula replied, looking straight ahead while Omega Jones shot a quick glance at Sulana through the rear-view mirror. It was almost as if he was expecting Sulana to react to the girl's statement. Sulana's lizard eyes remained steady while looking straight ahead at the road. She decided that she would not let on as to what she was really thinking. Still she pressed on.

"What is the organization's name?" Sulana asked, a few seconds later.

"It's called C.A.N.S., and it stands for Center for the Advancement of Noetic Sciences. It's an offshoot of the Philosophy Department at Centralia University."

They had descended about halfway into the valley by now, and Sulana could see that Ranes looked more like a town than a "reserve". A few structures bore a striking resemblance to typical buildings such as a fire department, hospital etc.

"Besides you and your friends, who else lives here?" queried Sulana further.

"There are quite a few professors and faculty members living here as well as some research scientists and a few lucky students such as myself and Omega here." Thula added, nodding toward him. "we're are lucky enough to be allowed to stay here while we attend Centralia U."

"I see. What is it that you're studying Mr. Jones?" Sulana asked, addressing the man for the first time.

"Please call me Omega or Om for short," he answered, smiling at her. "I'm working on my masters on Exo-Biology and I'm finishing my doctorate in Exo-Botany."

"Where do you plan to go after you receive your diplomas?"

"Back to my home world, Tegiran. It's a little-known planet a few parsecs from here where my skills are much needed," answered the man.

"I thought I detected a foreign accent in your speech. Your native tongue is Teduch is it not?"

"That is amazing!" exclaimed Omega. "Not many people know where my accent comes from or have ever heard of Teduch. You have an excellent ear for language Ms. Kay."

"Please call me Sulana and yes, Gulax ears are very sharp. Before I decided to become a historian I was going to study linguistics."

"Well it's never too late Sulana," Omega commented, smiling broadly. "Look at me. I'm sixty eight and I'm just graduating from college!"

"Indeed! Perhaps one day I'll go back to school and get a degree in languages." Sulana remarked.

The dirt road ended and became a two lane paved street. They had reached the valley's floor and Sulana noticed that the vegetation had changed dramatically. Gone were the small craggy bushes now replaced by beautiful trees and plants more commonly found on temperate and hot equatorial planets such as Earth or Tarsia. As they approached the outskirts, the first houses on the perimeter of the valley were now visible. After they passed a few, Sulana noticed how beautiful and lavish the architecture was on these homes. Some of them resembled the house she was staying in. As they came close to the center of town, the buildings became more impressive and majestic. The area reminded Sulana of the high-end neighborhoods commonly found in Western Europe and even some of the old mansions that once belonged to the Tarsian ruling class on T-Prime and Siraya, the old capital of the Kural. This town or "reserve", as Thula called it, looked as if it had been here for several centuries, not a hundred or so years which was when Centralia was colonized. She suspected that Professor Artemus was somehow involved in all this.

They reached the center of town which was comprised of a large circular park with a spacious lake in the middle. Sulana was surprised to see many of the inhabitants walking around in short sleeves and casual summer wear. Most were human, although a few other alien species could be seen here and there.

"Aren't they cold?" Sulana asked, almost to herself.

Thula smiled at her. "Hardly. The mean temperature here in the valley is eighty degrees Fahrenheit all year long."

"How is that possible?" questioned Sulana, knowing that Centralia was a sub-arctic planet located several hundred thousand miles further from its sun than Terra. It was the beginning of winter to boot!

"Well, Ranes is located on the lowest elevation on the entire planet, and it also happens to sit above a large network of hot springs that come down from the mountains to our west," Omega explained, pointing in that direction. "It's the only place on Centralia where the temperature reaches one hundred degrees in summer."

"Here I'll open the window," said Thula. "Here the air is warm and moist!"

Sulana held her breath fearing the worst. But then, a warm tropical-like breeze touched her face and she automatically peeled off the blankets from her body. She took a deep breath and the smell of a warm summer night such as she'd known in South Africa, hit her tongue, triggering memories of home.

"Remarkable!" was all she could say in her amazement.

The buggy left the center of town and was now climbing again, heading toward a large hill at the western end of the valley. Atop the hill, sat an impressive mansion. Its many windows glowing warmly in the night. The house was surrounded by other relatively smaller estates, all assembled inside a tall wrought-iron fence that circled the entire compound.

Sulana pointed toward the group of buildings now directly ahead. "Is that where we're going?" she asked, trying not to sound too impressed.

"Yes. That's the Center's headquarters and our house as well. Omega and I live in the 'big house' with some of our friends," Thula replied, turning to Sulana with a smile.

Sulana nodded and leaned back on her seat. She peeled off the last blanket by her legs and then took off her jacket. The buggy left the main road and drove through the main gate following a small circular drive that brought them to the front entrance of the house. Once there, Omega let the two females out and drove away following the driveway which curved around the house presumably leading to a parking lot. The entrance to the house was framed by four large columns of marbled granite under a cupola lit by a large lamp suspended in the middle of its ceiling. The double doors leading to the house were made of solid wood and were carved with Tarsian motifs. The architecture was impressive but not ostentatious.

Sulana turned and looked down at the valley floor from their vantage point on top of the hill. The town lights seemed to sparkle in the warmth of the shimmering evening air. On the south side of the valley, agro-machines illuminated by bright lights, tended to large fields growing a variety of crops. Looking northwards, Sulana could see a waterfall that fed a small river that wound its way through the center of town. The view was straight out of an artists' conception of what an idyllic landscape should look like. Sulana had been to many beautiful places on many planets in her life, but this place topped them all.

"It's beautiful isn't it?" Thula stated, interrupting Sulana's reverie.

"Yes, quite," Sulana replied.

"Come. Let's get inside. I'm anxious for you to meet the rest of my friends." Thula said, pulling her by her arm.

As they headed to the door. a large flyer came down for a landing somewhere in the rear of the house.

"That's probably Carlos, he commutes from the other side of the planet," Thula mentioned casually.

Once inside, Sulana found herself in a spacious circular atrium twenty meters high. In its center, a large three-tiered fountain sat surrounded by several varieties of large potted palm trees, flower beds and tropical plants. Behind the bubbling fountain, a large hall led to the center of the house. To the left and right, were two large rooms accessible through arched doorways. One, appeared to be an old-style library with thousands of books in shelves that reached as high as the atrium. The other, seemed to be some sort of large drawing room full of comfortable couches, sofas, coffee tables and a small bar. Both rooms appeared empty.

"Here, let me take your coat," Thula announced, taking Sulana's coat and putting it in a small cloak room to the right of the main doors.

Sulana stood there transfixed by the beauty of the atrium. Her tongue sampled the sweet smell of the plants kept moist by the evaporated water of the fountain. The combination of the sound of the water and the smell of the vegetation, reminded her of a place she knew long ago but couldn't remember now.

Taking Sulana once again by the arm, Thula gently coaxed her to follow her. "Let's go to the main kitchen. That's where everybody usually gathers."

Feeling like a child being led by an adult into a wonderland, Sulana let Thula take her further inside this spectacular home.

The hallway walls were framed by artwork originating from many places in the galaxy. Decorative vases and sculptures of every sort imaginable sat on tables beneath portraits of tenured professors and deans of the many departments of Centralia University. Several finely carved wooden doors along the path had metallic name plates of faculty and other staff members of the organization placed on them. The largest door near the end of the hall read: 'Dr. Zephron Artemus'.

Sulana smiled. Her hunch that the good professor was part of all this had been proven right.

At the end of the hallway Thula reached for a plain single door and opened it. A narrow curved stairway led down and Sulana had to follow single file. As they neared the bottom of the stairway, several voices could be heard carrying on a lively conversation. The smell of home cooked food wafted upwards into Sulana's tongue. She suddenly felt very hungry.

At the bottom of the stairs they reached a large kitchen. There, she saw Omega Jones, Vardik, (Thula's brother) and three other humans sitting around a large oval table brimming with food and drink.

"Everybody!" announced Thula addressing the group. "This is Sulana Kay, the professor's guest who I've been telling you about!"

All five members stood up and circled Sulana welcoming her to the house. The fact that she was Gulax did not seem to affect the warmth and camaraderie that these people were showing her. They seemed genuinely happy to meet her.

A burly man in his thirties named Carlos with a pleasant round face, framed by a tussle of black hair and green eyes, introduced Sulana to the other two that she hadn't met before. One, was Terence a tall handsome young man with deep blue eyes and long dark pony tail and the other was Susan, a short attractive woman in her forties with auburn hair and blue eyes. None of them appeared to be related to one another. Yet, they all shared something similar. Sulana made a mental note.

"Are you hungry Sulana?" asked Susan, pointing to the table.

"Now that you mentioned it, yes I am. I could use some nourishment."

Omega Jones came around the table with an extra chair and placed it in front of Sulana.

"Sit yourself down and grab whatever you like. We don't stand on ceremony in this house," he offered gleefully.

Carlos grabbed some silverware and Vardik brought plates, a glass and a cloth napkin to the table. Sulana was glad to see that most of the food on the table was vegetarian. She filled her plate with food and ate the delicious fare with gusto. She felt warm and comfortable and realized that she hadn't felt this hungry since she'd arrived in Centralia.

While the others were clearing the dishes and washing utensils, Thula sat next to Sulana and put her arm around her. "You seem to be enjoying the food Sulana. Are you comfortable? Is the temperature to your liking?"

In between bites Sulana nodded her approval. Terence announced that he was making a big pot of green tea. "Would you like some tea also?" he asked Sulana.

Sulana said yes, and after she finished eating, everyone sat back at the table to partake in the tea. The conversation became quieter but still remained lively.

"Carlos here owns the biggest flyer in the group. We can always tell when he's arriving by the thunder of his engines!" Thula explained laughing, while the others joined her in teasing their friend.

"Don't pay attention to these people!" Carlos protested in jest. "They're all jealous because their flyers can't go above the atmosphere like mine can."

Terence interjected. "Carlos works in Planitia Valley on the other side of the planet."

"What do you do over there Carlos?" Sulana asked.

"I'm a terraforming engineer. I'm overseeing the last sequence of ocean development on Centralia. The job should be finished in about thirty years or so."

"How wonderful!" Sulana exclaimed. "My parents are both terraformers and I lived on Zelah Secundus for a year while they served there."

"I knew I liked you for a reason!" Carlos responded with his perfect white teeth forming a big smile. "Any child of a terraformer is a friend of mine," he concluded, smirking at the others.

"Carlos thinks that Terence and I look down upon him because he only has one doctorate." Susan added, winking at Carlos with a crooked smile.

"Oh shush!" he interrupted her, dismissing the two of them with a wave of his hand. "Your degrees are all in obscure specialties like Inter-dimensional Dynamics, Time dilation Physics and Super Conductive Biometrics!" he shot back, displaying mock anger at Susan. "And You!" he continued, now aiming his friendly ridicule at Terence. "You are the poster boy for lovey-dovey fluffy doctorates. Listen to this Sulana," he complained, seemingly incensed. Dr. of Theosophy, Philosophy and Psychology! Can you believe these two?" he expounded, shaking his head in pretend disbelief. "The two of them put together have not done an honest day's work in their entire lives! Whereas I, I work for a living!" he concluded, as everyone applauded his dramatic performance.

Even Sulana who was normally immune to humor, let out a quiet hiss under her breath.

Thula leaned against her and held her arm as she convulsed with laughter with the others. Suddenly Sulana caught the scent of her hair and felt a strong moment of déjà vu. The feeling came and went quickly, but it left the lingering sensation of a forgotten memory. She became dizzy and had to close her eyes for a moment.

The laughter quieted down and Sulana found herself being quietly observed by the others.

"Are you alright Sulana?" asked Omega, looking concerned. The others looked away and continued talking. The old man came around the table and sat next to her.

"It's very strange," she said softly. "I just experienced what I can only refer to as a moment of déjà vu."

"Is that unusual for you? asked Omega.

"Very!" Sulana whispered. "Lizards do not experience déjà vu."

"And yet here you are," he stated, while looking critically at Thula.

Without Sulana noticing, Thula looked down sheepishly and gently let go of Sulana's arm.

"Don't worry about it my dear. It's probably due to all the excitement brought about by these crazy bohemians," he assured her, nodding at the others.

"Hey everybody, why don't we go upstairs to the music room so we can stretch out and relax more comfortably?" Proposed Carlos.

"Sounds like a great idea. Why don't you all go up. Thula and I will stay here to finish cleaning up," Omega suggested, looking straight at Thula.

The group left with Sulana in tow.

As the sound of the steps of the other four faded in the narrow stairway, Omega turned to Thula.

"Thula, I know that you want to speed up the process," he began, gesturing up at the floor above. I've warned you that if you push her, she could be hurt emotionally or worse psychologically. You wouldn't wish that on her, would you?" he asked, looking intently into Thula's eyes. "Remember that she is Gulax," he continued. "she might not be ready."

"I feel it in my heart that she is Om, I really do!" Responded Thula emphatically. "I don't want to wait!"

"Then, by all that is holy in this universe, slow down and let the process take its own course!"

"You're right Om, I'm letting my impatience and my desire nature get in the way. I won't push her anymore, I promise." she whispered, fighting back tears.

"Maybe in another ten thousand years or so you might learn patience as I had to," he joked affectionately, as he wrapped his arms around Thula's thin frame, holding her gently.

They stood embracing for a few more seconds then separated and went about cleaning the rest of the dirty dishes left on the table.

CHAPTER 4

Remembrance

Up in the music room, Sulana and the others were enjoying themselves watching Carlos' antics as he performed a funny dance with Susan to an ancient song played by a marching band from Earth. Carlos was the clown of the group and she could see that the others liked to be entertained by him, even though they pretended to be embarrassed by his crass humor. Muscular and stocky, he was the quintessential everyman that drunk a little too much and laughed a little too loud at parties, but everyone always invited him along because he livened up everyone's spirits.

In contrast, Terence's demeanor was that of a quiet gentle studious man who probably preferred to spend a quiet evening at home reading a book on the nature of consciousness or some other similar intellectual tome. Yet, his eyes occasionally flashed with the glint of a subdued mischievous individual held back by social convention.

Thula's brother Vardik was more of a mystery. As she'd observed earlier in the day, he acted very regal and dignified. His royal bearing almost made one want to curtsy when he entered a room. He would participate with the group but only at a distance.

Susan on the other hand was warm and friendly and her eyes told you that she loved people. She looked like she was somebody's typical mom. It was easy to imagine her taking the kids to school, cleaning house and cooking for the family. If you'd just met her you would never guess that she held three doctorates in highly esoteric advanced physics.

Sulana turned toward the music room's door expecting to see Thula and Omega come up from the kitchen anytime soon. She liked the old man's gentle personality. His kind eyes showed infinite wisdom and at the same time a kind of melancholy that comes from having lived a very contemplative life. Perhaps, he'd been a monk in some religious order. Yes! He definitely could have been a priest or a father superior in some monastery.

She suddenly felt as if she had known these people for many years. The way they had welcomed her to the house and their genuine show of affection for her had softened Sulana's heart very quickly. They treated her as a family would treat one of its own members. These people exhibited no guile or put on airs of any kind. Their behavior was open and natural. Sulana reflected on all this and her mind flashed back to Thula's invitation earlier that day to come visit her at the 'house'. She had said; "We're more like a family than anything else and I think that you'd enjoy meeting them."

Sulana found herself wishing for the first time in her life that her parents could have given her a sister to grow up with. Unfortunately, it was very rare for Gulax couples to bear more than one offspring. She looked back at the door, and her heart jumped when she saw Thula's face appear as she entered the room. Without thinking about it, she got up from her sofa and walked up to her. This time she grabbed Thula's arm and gently pulled her back to the sofa. "You were down there so long. You two must have cleaned every pot and pan in the place!" Sulana commented.

"We share the house with five other people so the kitchen is sacred territory. Whoever uses the kitchen must leave it as he or she found it. Those are house rules!"

"Now that I've met some of your wonderful friends I'm anxious to meet the rest. Tell me about them!" Sulana demanded excitedly.

"Let's see, Waldo you've already met. Then there's Carlatta, Faruk, Matilda and Tuli. Tuli is the youngest. She's a ten-year-old genius working on her masters in astrophysics. She's a Tareean and went back to Taree for their holiday season. You'll meet her soon. I think she's coming back next week." Thula paused and turned to Terence. "Have you seen Faruk today?"

"Yes, but he's been in his room all day. He's caught a cold, so I don't think we'll see him downstairs for a while."

Turning back to Sulana, Thula continued. "Faruk's the oldest. He's ninety-seven. He's getting on in years and lately he's been in poor health so we all take turns looking after the poor dear. He's the first one of us all to have moved into the house when Ranes was first settled almost a hundred years ago. After he received his doctorate in literature, he became a professor at Centralia U and has always worked for the college. He retired several years ago. I believe that he's lived here most of his life."

"Remarkable!" Sulana commented, wondering why the man chose to live in only one place most of his adult life.

"And last but not least, there's Matilda." Thula added, her eyes smiling with obvious affection. She's my dearest friend. We grew up together in T Prime and have attended the same schools together since childhood. She stays at professor Artemus' house up in the mountains for days on end. She's been helping the professor finish a multivolume encyclopedia on Galactic Civilizations that he's been working on for years. She also should be back next week." Thula paused and put her hand on Sulana's shoulder affectionately. "You remind me very much of Matilda. I think you'll both get along famously when you two meet."

"What an interesting and varied group of people you are!" Sulana remarked, dazzled by the description of the five missing members of the 'family'.

"And of course, then there is you my dear Sulana!" Thula added happily. "Wouldn't it be wonderful if you could live with us as well?" she proposed with a note of hope in her voice. "Perhaps after you finish your dissertation you could move to Centralia and come to work at the University. I'm sure professor Artemus could find a position for you in the History Department," she added enthusiastically.

What Thula was proposing was so far from what Sulana had planned for her life. Yet, she found her pulse quickening at the idea of becoming part of this unusual group of individuals.

"Goodness gracious Thula!" Sulana said, exhaling softly. "Your invitation is most tempting. I can almost see myself living here amongst you and sharing my life with you all. Barely two weeks ago I was sitting in my hotel room running out of money and waiting for an interview with Professor Artemus." Sulana paused to take a deep breath. "I'm a little overwhelmed by all that has transpired in the past forty-eight hours. I'm afraid that I can't consider your kind invitation to join your group right now. I hope you'll forgive me. Perhaps in the future I might consider it."

Sulana could not help but see the disappointment in the young girl's eyes though she put on a brave front to hide it.

"I'm sorry," Thula said demurely, lowering her eyes and looking apologetic. "I'm always rushing things. It's terrible having to live in a young body!" she complained with seeming frustration. "My mind is patient and disciplined, but my body is always in a hurry and its chemistry betrays me in inconvenient ways."

"I know what you mean Thula!" Sulana responded, understanding how sometimes her own impatient nature got the best of her. She identified easily with Thula's constant struggle between patience and discipline and the impetuous nature of youth. "It is that very weakness in me that pushed me to break the law back on Plantanimus last year!" she admitted, lowering her voice.

"Sulana please forget that I just asked you to stay with us. I want you to enjoy your stay in Centralia. I shouldn't have put you in such a spot. And you're right, you must finish your work before you can even consider such a major decision."

Sulana was about to respond to Thula's words when Omega walked up to them.

"Hey you two!" he announced. "We're all going to the green house to look at my night blooming orchids. They open their beautiful petals only one night during the year and tonight's the night," he added, excitedly. "Sulana, you in particular should see this!" he offered, motioning to Thula and Sulana to join him and the others.

They followed arm in arm and exited the music room through a different door from the one that led to the kitchen. The door revealed a secondary hallway leading to the rear of the mansion.

As they headed to what appeared to be another atrium at the end of the hall, the group passed by several rooms on both sides of the long passage that appeared to be scientific labs full of technology. This part of the house looked more like a state of the art research center than anything else. One large room had the appearance of a medical facility.

Sulana's questioning eyes prompted Thula to explain. "Through the university, C.A.N.S. offers several grants to scientists working in many areas of research and it maintains a fulltime medical staff to care for anyone working here. That includes those who live in the house as well."

"How many people are involved in all this work?" Sulana wondered.

"All together, there are about a thousand people including support staff. Most of them live in the other houses in the compound."

"I see... who else besides the ten of you lives in the house?" Sulana queried, already knowing the answer.

"It's just the ten of us. I guess we're lucky that we don't have to share our living quarters with anyone else." Thula answered casually, avoiding Sulana's eyes.

"Lucky indeed." Sulana remarked, aware that the girl was hiding something. The more she got to know these people, the more questions kept popping up in her mind. She began to get the feeling that she was being tested in some subtle way. But why? Sulana asked herself. Thula seemed keen to have her join the group and live with them in this luxurious palatial state located in an isolated tropical paradise in the middle of a sub-arctic planet.

A twentieth century Terran story about a mythical place located high in the Himalayan Mountains called 'Shangri La', came to her mind. In the story, a man escaping an armed conflict from a country called China, becomes stranded in the Himalayas when the flying vessel that he was traveling in, crash-lands in the mountains. He and the other passengers are rescued and taken to a warm and temperate valley where they take refuge. While there, they discover that any ailments or chronic diseases that they had before coming to Shangri La have healed or disappeared. Shangri La is run by a Lama or "high priest" who is several hundred years old and has reached that age due to the valley's life prolonging magical properties. The Lama however, is finally near the end of his life and asks the man to stay and take over his position. The man foolishly decides to leave and go back to his more modern civilization. When he leaves he takes with him a beautiful young woman who had lived in Shangri La for many years with whom he had fallen in love. But as soon as they leave the valley's border, she ages incredibly fast and dies from old age in a matter of minutes. Through a complicated set of circumstances, he eventually returns and takes over the Lama's position and finds peace.

"Did you ever hear of Shangri La?" Sulana asked Thula, as they were about to reach the green house. "It's from an old story called Lost Horizons."

"Shangri La?" Thula responded, showing that the question had stirred some emotion.

"Yes, Shangri La." Sulana repeated, puzzled by the girl's reaction to her question.

"Yes… yes I'm familiar with that tale," Thula admitted, looking straight ahead. She seemed to be searching for the right words to say. She suddenly stopped walking and looked to the side in a funny way. "My parents used to tell me that story when I was a child. I hadn't thought about it in a long time. What made you think of it?" she asked, turning back to Sulana with a searching look.

"I'm not sure." Sulana said pensively, sensing that she shouldn't say too much. "Something about this house and this beautiful valley made me think about it."

"Interesting," muttered Thula under her breath. "You know, that used to be one of my favorite bedtime stories when I was very young."

"Really? You know, at its heart, that story is an object lesson about knowing when you've found something good in your life and not letting go of it because of ignorance."

"How true that is Sulana, how true that is." Thula agreed, softly.

Sulana and Thula had stopped at the threshold of the entrance to the green house which was a smaller version of the atrium at the front of the mansion. To Sulana's delight, the green house was much hotter than the interior of the house. The huge space was semicircular in shape and ahead, Sulana could see several dozen flower beds and many exotic plants and trees illuminated solely by the light of the bright stars in the Centralian night sky. In the eerie light under the giant curved glass ceiling, the place looked like an enchanted forest. Behind the green house lay a large manicured garden with a narrow stream running through its center that flowed towards the house.

The grounds were decorated with neatly trimmed hedges extending several meters away from the house rising slightly up the hill and culminating in a waterfall that fed the stream as it met with the house's spacious landing pad above the waterfall.

Beyond that, the terrain rose sharply and became a mountain range. The effect was spectacular and Sulana wondered if at some point she might become immune to so much beauty all in one place.

Near the center of the greenhouse, the silhouetted figures of the others, motioned them to hurry up. Making their way through the foliage, Sulana and Thula joined the others who were gathered around a large table filled with flowerpots. They stood in silence under the light of the stars, lending the moment a feeling of ceremony.

Sulana's ears noticed that the group's individual heartbeats were raised in anticipation of the event. Omega's heart seemed to beat faster than the others. She was ready for something out of the ordinary. When it happened, she wasn't disappointed.

Almost imperceptibly at first, and then more obviously, all the bulbs began opening as if on cue. After a few seconds, all the flowers on the table opened their white petals widely, exposing their green stamens, whose tips began to glow a light fluorescent blue and then turned to a soft pink. A collective sigh was heard around the table and at the same time, Thula's hand tightened around Sulana's arm with excitement. Within seconds, a sweet minty scent began flowing from the flowers and the sound of nostrils inhaling the fragrance went around the table. Sulana immediately stuck her tongue out joining the others in the experience. She had smelled flowers all through her life, but this was the most exquisite perfume she had ever known. To her surprise, her heart was beating as fast as the others. She looked around the table and observed the look of wonder in everyone's eyes, including Vardik, whose regal expression had temporarily morphed into that of a fascinated child. Sulana noticed that Omega's own experience must have been very deep for him because the old man's eyes were filled with tears.

"Thank you everyone for sharing this moment with me," he said with voice full of emotion. "I've been breeding these beauties for many years, and tonight was by far the most spectacular blooming I've seen with this species."

"I'll say!" Sulana said with reverence.

"I'm so glad that you were here with us to witness this rare moment Sulana!" the old man said his voice breaking a little.

Sulana reached for the man's shoulder affectionately initiating physical contact which was unusual for her. "I don't think that I'll ever forget this night for the rest of my life Omega," Sulana stated honestly.

"Thank you my dear. It means a lot to me to hear you say that!" he answered gratefully.

Sulana looked back at the table and was shocked to see that all the flowers had quickly withered and turned dark brown. She looked at Omega questioningly.

"Yes." he said smiling, with a bittersweet expression. "The last few minutes of life is the most spectacular and beautiful moment of their existence," he added with a hint of sadness. "But don't feel too bad. Within their withered remains, they hold the seeds for the next generation. By spring, this table will be full of new life again."

"Now I understand what you meant by 'witnessing this rare moment' Omega," commented Sulana with awe.

"Quite so my dear. If you'll excuse me, I must retrieve the seeds from their remains to dry them quickly. Otherwise they'll spoil."

Omega went back to the table and began collecting the dead flowers in a flat tray.

"Would you like to see the garden with me?" Thula suggested, tilting her head in that direction. "I'm sure it's still warm outside."

Sulana agreed and zipped up her coveralls. When they stepped outside, she was glad to find the temperature was still a balmy eighty degrees Fahrenheit. The two of them walked uphill along the stream without speaking. The sound of the water gurgling as it made its way downhill, sounded like music to her ears.

Below the waterfall, the water collected in a large pool lit by artificial lights from below. To the right of the pool, sat a round gazebo made of wrought iron with marble benches inside. The two went in and sat down next to each other.

They remained silent, not saying anything, just admiring the beautiful view and listening to the roar of the waterfall. The light from the pool illuminated the spray of the water as it floated up disappearing into the black sky. Once again, Sulana experienced a strong sense of déjà vu. A feeling that she had been in a place very much like this once before, kept tugging at her. Like an elusive word or a name at the tip of your tongue.

Breaking the silence, Sulana spoke. "You know, if I were human, I would say that this place is magical and that it casts a spell on those who enter its boundaries."

Thula who had been looking at the waterfall turned to her with a curious look in her eyes. "What makes you say that?"

"There's something about this house and this valley that feels different from any other place that I've ever been before, with the exception of Plantanimus."

Thula raised her eyebrows and widened her eyes. Her heartbeat began to rise. "Is that so?" she said, steadying her voice.

"Yes. When I was on Plantanimus last year I experienced a similar kind of elation which I attributed to the fact that I was making headway in my research and that in some way I felt honored to be walking the same sacred ground that gave birth to the Dreamers, Kelem, Anima and the rest. The difference between the two places is that Plantanimus felt like a place that was once imbued with the energy of a powerful spirit but had sadly dissipated. My colleagues felt it more than I but despite my Gulax nature, I too became aware of that feeling. We likened it to the memory of a beautiful symphony lingering in the minds of the audience after the performance is over. Dr. Gurwat called it a kind of melancholy. Like a feeling of loss, or a sense of missed opportunities."

Sulana paused and became quiet. She took a deep breath, searching for the right words.

She turned and looked at the beautiful garden grounds, the green house at the rear of the main house surrounded by the smaller houses in the compound and the valley below. Her voice sounding oddly distant. "But here…I feel like I'm sitting in the middle of the orchestra during the concert and beautiful music is playing all around me, and I don't want it to stop. And I'm afraid that if it were to stop I could not bear it. You see Thula, that must be the way the spell works! As long as I stay here, I'm under its influence and the symphony goes on. But the moment I leave, all that remains is the memory of the music." She looked up at the stars shimmering from the warm air currents rising from the valley and continued. "I think this place is my Shangri La Thula! And I'm afraid that I'm going to leave this place just like the foolish man in the story who left paradise because of his ignorance."

Thula's heart and mind became overwhelmed with emotion. "So close, so close and yet she doesn't see what's right in front of her!" Thula shouted in her mind. Then, while Sulana remained looking down at the valley, she got up from the bench and ran to the edge of the waterfall. She didn't want Sulana to see her crying. She couldn't let her know how upset she was, it could ruin everything! Omega had warned her not to push Sulana, but this time Thula hadn't done anything. Sulana was obviously breaking through the veil on her own and Thula knew that this was the most delicate moment in the process. Any hint that Sulana's growing awareness was causing Thula to feel so vulnerable and emotional could send Sulana into an emotional freeze that would cancel any chance of her remembering who she was!

Sulana felt strangely liberated by having told Thula how this place made her feel. Something was stirring in her and that something had opened a door that allowed her to express herself in a way that she had never done before. It both frightened her and at the same time made her want to dig deeper within herself and reveal whatever it was that was bringing about this change in her awareness.

She sensed something had shifted, and turning around, realized that Thula had left the gazebo and was now standing by the waterfall facing away from her.

Concerned she went to Thula. "Is everything alright?" she asked, wondering if she had said something to upset the young girl.

"I'm fine." Thula replied, still facing the waterfall. "It doesn't have to be that way you know," Thula said quietly, her voice barely audible over the sound of the water. "The symphony is playing no matter where you are. And although this place is very special, it's the people that love you and care for you that create the kind of magic that you're talking about."

"You're right. When I was comparing this place to Plantanimus, I was speaking somewhat metaphorically, but I must admit not entirely. Ever since I came to Centralia and met Professor Artemus and you and the rest of your friends, I've been experiencing some unusual things. I can't explain it, but something in me has changed and I'm not sure what it all means."

Thula turned around and faced Sulana with a neutral expression, though her eyes betrayed a hidden sadness.

"You're probably overwhelmed by all the things that have happened since your arrival and it's true that my friends and I are a bit too much to take all at once. I hope that you're having a good time despite the busy social schedule," Thula added, smiling bravely.

"I am Thula. I am having a good time and I really like you and your wonderful friends."

"I'm glad Sulana. Whatever happens I hope that we can stay friends forever." Sulana reached and hugged her new found friend with tender affection. A cool breeze came down from the mountain and Sulana shivered. Thula noticed the Gulax's reaction to the temperature change.

"I think we better get you back to the house," Thula suggested.

"I thought you said that it stays warm all year round," Sulana complained, a little disappointed.

"Well that's for most of the day. but in wintertime, around 3-8, the winds come down from the west over the mountain range and cool the valley until sunrise."

"How cold does it get?" Sulana asked, as they walked downhill back to the house.

"Oh, about sixty degrees Fahrenheit."

"That's plenty cold for me!" Sulana thought, as she picked up her pace and ran for the door to the green house.

The green house was now empty and quiet under the starry night. Everyone had gone back to the house and the place still vibrated with its magical quality in Sulana's perception. She looked at the empty pots on the table and the memory of the night blooming orchids came flooding back to her with a rush of images and the smell of the flower's potent perfume. It was almost as if she was reliving the event. Sulana tasted the air with her tongue and thought she could still detect a few random molecules of the flower's scent still floating in the air, but it was most likely her highly developed olfactory gland that was playing tricks with her mind. In a flash of understanding she recognized the similarity between the memory of the dying orchids' perfume and the melancholy feeling that she and her colleagues had experienced on Plantanimus as the echoes of a beautiful symphony. She suddenly felt a wave of sadness and regret such as she'd never experienced before. The emotion grew in intensity until it made her feel like she was going to pass out.

Thula, who was a step or two behind her, caught her by the shoulders as Sulana's legs buckled and managed to let her slide gently to the floor. Sulana was struggling to understand what was happening to her, and soon afterwards, her mind shut down. Her body went limp in Thula's arms.

Thula panicked and screamed for help, quickly realizing that no one could hear her from the green house. She lay Sulana's head down gently on the floor and ran to the hallway to call the others on the house's intercom.

She alerted the others and ran back to Sulana. She kneeled and cradled her gently in her arms as her eyes filled with tears. She began to rock her back and forth as one would a sick child. Within moments, Carlos, Terence and Susan came running and gasped, when they saw Sulana's body on the floor. In one quick motion, Carlos slid down to the floor and easily picked up Sulana's wiry frame in his muscular arms.

He carried her to the infirmary a few doors down the hallway. Susan and Terence lifted Thula from the floor. The girl seemed near collapse herself.

"What happened Thula?" the two of them asked in unison.

"I… I don't know! We had just returned from the garden and she stopped to look at the table where the orchids were, and then she started shaking and collapsed!"

"Thula! We warned you not to 'push' her. Why didn't you listen to us? Terence said, trying not to badger her under the circumstances.

"You don't understand I wasn't pushing her. Not after Om told me to stop when we were in the kitchen. She's breaking through the veil on her own. I had nothing to do with it this time." As Susan and Terence led Thula back to the hallway, they exchanged worried glances.

When they walked into the infirmary, Omega was already connecting nano leads to Sulana who lay unconscious in one of the med-beds. Three medics that been summoned by Carlos through the compound's intercom appeared at the door. One of them was still putting on his trousers. Within minutes, they were ministering to Sulana with an array of medical equipment.

Staying out of the way, Thula, Susan and Terence stood by the door, watching helplessly as Omega and the medics tried to make sense of Sulana's condition.

A while later, Omega walked over to where the three were standing.

"Call Zephron, Waldo and Carlatta and tell them to come here right away!

Carlos ran out the door as soon as Omega spoke. Thula sank into despair and Susan walked her over to some chairs out in the hall.

Thula put her head on Susan's lap and began to cry.

CHAPTER 5

Prognosis and Therapy For Sulana

The meeting room in the second floor of the mansion faced the rear of the house. The waterfall at the end of the garden and the mountain behind it were becoming visible as the morning sun rising over the valley's eastern border colored everything a deep orange.

Five individuals sat around a conference table. A single Tiffany lamp suspended above the center of its oval shaped oak surface was the only light in the room.

"There's nothing physiologically wrong with her," Omega said, looking at the others.

"I'm sure you're right Om. The thing is, how should we proceed next?" commented professor Artemus, sitting to his right.

The group became silent again. Their somber faces reflected their troubled minds.

"I experienced something similar when I was young back on Mars if you all remember," Waldo commented, breaking the silence."

"Yes, my boy, but that incident was not caused by psychological trauma but by your latent ability as a medical empath, was it not?" reflected the professor.

"True. But there are symptomatic similarities in both cases, and we might be able to treat Sulana's condition with the same technique that I was treated with."

"Enlighten me, my darling. I don't share the same memories that you do with Zephron and Omega," asked a stunningly beautiful brunette with green eyes seated next to Waldo.

"I'm sorry Carlatta. I forget sometimes that I didn't know you until my thirties," Waldo said apologetically, smiling at the green-eyed dark-haired beauty sitting next to him. "When I was sixteen, I fell into a coma almost at the same time that my aunt Margarita collapsed unconscious from a brain tumor. We were both hospitalized and the doctors diagnosed my aunt's condition right away but they couldn't figure out why I remained in a comatose state. They ran a battery of tests on me but couldn't find anything physically wrong with me as in Sulana's case. Fortunately for me, my old friend, Professor Nicolas Alfano, a very gifted psychic along with two of his colleagues, cured me by performing a procedure where they entered a deep meditative state and joined their consciousness with my own. They then 'appeared' inside my subconscious mind construct and very skillfully 'awakened' me from my dreaming state. Thus, ending my coma."

"And you think that we could help Sulana the same way?" asked Carlos, sitting at the far end of the conference table.

Waldo was about to answer when Omega interrupted him. "Not so fast Carlito," he interrupted, using the diminutive form in Spanish affectionately. "Sulana is a Gulax and we don't have any experience dealing with her species. We could go inside her subconscious and cause more harm."

"But we have to do something!" pleaded Carlatta, holding on to Waldo's arm.

"Of course, we're going to do everything in our power to help her, but we must proceed with great caution. We're treading on unknown territory here," warned the professor.

Carlatta leaned her head on Waldo's shoulder. "The poor dear. All these years away from us and now that she's come back to us, this terrible thing happens!"

"Be of good cheer my love. We've overcome bigger challenges than this many times before," Waldo reassured her, putting his arm around her shoulder.

"Dear ones," Professor Artemus said, looking kindly at Carlos, Waldo and Carlatta. "Please know that Omega and I are as worried as you are," he said, nodding to his left. "We've known all of you throughout your many lives, and her absence has deeply affected us as well."

"We all know that professor, so let's stop talking about how bad we feel about poor Tar..., I mean Sulana and let's do something to help her!" Carlos suggested impatiently. He had almost used Sulana's old name.

"You're right Carlos. Let's concentrate on a solution. I propose that we devise a similar therapeutic treatment as was given to me on Mars," Waldo proposed confidently.

"That sounds good. I vote for that!" Carlos agreed, energetically.

Omega leaned back in his chair and looked at Waldo, then nodded in agreement, though somewhat reluctantly. "Fine how do we go about it?"

"You and Omega have always been capable of communicating with all of us telepathically," Waldo said, looking at the professor and Omega. "Thula is your equal in ability and me and Carlatta are a close second." He paused and looked at Carlos apologetically. "Sorry Carlito, I would include you in the mix, but your telepathy is hit-and-miss and it could cause problems in this situation."

"No offense taken, Waldo. I know my limitations." Carlos responded with a friendly grin.

"I'm concerned about Thula." Omega said, with a worried look on his brow. "She's been hit harder emotionally than all of us and I'm not sure that even if this procedure is workable, that it would be a good idea to include her in treating Sulana."

"I wish that she'd consulted with us before planting that silly book of poems in that bookstore in Montevideo!" interjected Professor Artemus, with frustration.

"What's done is done Zephron," Carlatta said. "Thula never got over Tarsia's disappearance and besides, what did you expect her to do when she discovered that we had found her sister after more than four hundred years?"

71

Carlatta had spoken out loud Sulana's previous incarnation name and she didn't care. For security and privacy reasons, in 2965 after leaving Plantanimus, they had all decided to use different names, even amongst themselves, each time they were born in a new body. But Carlatta still thought of herself as Anima and Waldo would forever be Kelem to her, no matter their physical appearance. She hated having to call everyone by a different name each time they were reborn. She shared Thula's (once Tatiana) pain from the loss of her older sister Tarsia (now Sulana).

Tatiana and Tarsia had been extremely close. They were the youngest of the Rogeston children and they spent the most time together while growing up. However, after Tarsia left Plantanimus she never returned. She of all the ten Rogeston children, protested and fought the hardest to remain in Plantanimus. When she was finally forced to leave at age seventeen so that she could gain wisdom and learn about the world outside of Plantanimus, she felt betrayed and abandoned and never forgave the family for exiling her from paradise. Carlatta knew that the trauma of that event damaged Tarsia so deeply that it kept her from returning home.

For the last four hundred and thirty-six years, the first thing that Tatiana always asked in each incarnation, as soon as her new body would allow her to speak, was; "Has my sister been found?"

"Can we get back to the business at hand?" demanded Carlos with irritation, snapping Carlatta out of her introspection. "Why or how Thula did what she did, is not the issue before us."

"You're right Carlos, sorry for digressing. Now Waldo, what are the risks involved in this procedure? Professor Artemus asked.

"The risk is that of one or more of us possibly getting lost inside the subject's Lower Mental Body's 'construct world'. That's why professor Alfano, the strongest mind of the three individuals, acted as 'safety control'. Aways keeping the other two individuals from getting caught inside my mind."

Waldo then looked at professor Artemus. "Zephron, you have the strongest mind of us all. I suppose that should be your job. Om, you should take point, since you are the strongest after Zephron. And then

Carlatta and I, and possibly Thula, if we decide to include her. But only as a backup.

"Sounds relatively simple in theory. But how can we prepare to do this without a run through or some sort of rehearsal?" Omega asked, concerned.

"There's only one way," Waldo said, and then he looked at Carlos. 'We need a volunteer."

Professor Artemus Omega and Carlatta looked first at Carlos, whose surprised expression spoke volumes. They turned to Waldo with surprise.

He knew that his statement had shocked everyone, but he had to remain strong. "Well, if not Carlos, then Susan or Terence," he added, spreading his hands.

"What about Vardik, why not include him in the list of potential guinea pigs? Carlos suggested sarcastically.

Waldo leaned on the table and placed his chin in his hands. "Vardik appears to be struggling with egotism in this particular incarnation, though I have great hopes for him, once his young body matures."

"I really don't want Susan or Terence involved in all this!" Carlos said, worried for his siblings.

"I'm curious. Why did you pick Carlos first and not one of the others?" Omega asked Waldo.

Waldo leaned back in his chair and looked at Carlos affectionately. "Because Carlos is Carlos! Of all of us, he's always known exactly what he wants out of life no matter what the circumstances are in each incarnation. He never lacks confidence or a sense of direction. Since I've known him as Dario back on Plantanimus, he's always had the ability to remain true to his nature. His telepathy may be less than perfect, but his mind is as solid as steel. That's why I looked in his direction when I said we needed a volunteer."

Carlos looked down smiling knowing that his grandfather had spoken the truth.

"I'll do it," he said, looking at the others with confidence. "How long will you all be rattling around inside my mind?"

"Only a few minutes. We only need to know how it feels to enter a person's mental substructure as a group. Once we learn from the experience, we can proceed with Sulana." Waldo answered.

"Will I be awake during this time?" asked Carlos.

"We'll put you in a semiconscious meditative state similar to how it felt when you communed with Zephron and Omega when they were Dreamers. Once you reach that state, you will not be aware of our presence since we'll be operating in the 'unconscious' part of your mind."

"Fine let's do it. When do we start?" Carlos said, ready at the go.

"Hold on cowboy!" Waldo said laughing. "First, none of us got any sleep last night," he added, pointing at the garden and the mountain behind the mansion, now basking in the morning sun. "We should all get eight hours of sleep at least, and then we'll conduct our run through tonight when it's psychically quieter than in the daytime. Then, if we don't run into any problems, we will decide when to minister to Sulana."

Carlos got up from his chair and headed for the door. "I have to contact my crew in Planitia Valley and tell them that I won't be back for a day or two."

"Fine and get some sleep right after that!" Waldo shouted, as Carlos left the room.

"I pray that you'll all be safe," Carlatta whispered with concern for her friends.

"We'll take every precaution my love and as you said earlier, we must do something!" Waldo said holding Carlatta tightly in his arms.

Zephron Artemus rose from his chair and stretched his long frame. "Well young man, we're all going to sleep as you ordered, but you should follow your own advice and head for bed yourself."

"Aye, aye captain!" Waldo responded, bringing his hand to his forehead in a mock military salute.

Omega, Waldo and Carlatta stood up and followed the professor as he exited the room.

Waldo and Carlatta headed for their bedroom as Omega and Zephron went to theirs.

A few minutes later, Waldo lay on his bed unable to fall asleep. Carlatta was already snoring gently, her left arm wrapped around his chest. He envied her ability to always fall asleep soundly no matter what was going on in their life. Hard as he tried however, sleep wouldn't come. He was worried about Sulana and the possible effect that the procedure could have on her mind and body. He was also worried about Thula and the personality quirks that had manifested in her character in this current incarnation. For the first time in nearly four hundred years since her life as Tatiana, Thula was having trouble controlling her emotions. Four centuries ago, after she returned to Plantanimus, she became the strength and center of the family. She was the one that managed to regroup the Rogeston Clan (minus Tarsia) and found a way to transfer everyone's consciousness into humanoid bodies, thus saving the Dreamers from oblivion. But as Thula, she had become emotionally dependent on everyone else.

Zephron, Omega and Waldo had tried to help her regain her old strength and confidence, but her young body's brain chemistry seemed to hold her back. From early childhood, she had become obsessed with finding Tarsia and returning her to the Rogeston Clan. Through deep meditation, Zephron found that Tarsia's soul had incarnated in the body of Sulana Kay. He made Waldo and Omega aware of that fact. The three of them began to plan a way to bring her back to their midst. But Thula accidentally found out about Zephron's discovery and took matters into her own hands by planting Zeus' book of poetry in a bookstore in Montevideo on Earth, knowing that it would lead Sulana to Centralia.

The three men had wanted to use a more patient and deliberate way to bring Sulana back to the group. But once Thula had acted, they had to become complicit in her scheme, despite their misgivings. Still, they thought that with care and patience they could help Sulana remember her old life once she arrived in Centralia. But unfortunately, Thula's undisciplined psychic "pushing" had caused Sulana to go into shock upon remembering her old identity before she was ready.

Now Thula had fallen into a deep depression and had become nearly catatonic. She realized that she had caused Sulana's "psychic shock coma" and was racked with guilt. After they helped Sulana, she would need their help next.

Waldo's sixteen-year-old body was not immune to the brain chemistry of youth either. Despite his seven hundred years of life experience and several re-incarnations, he was having difficulty maintaining his equanimity and even temper under the current stressful circumstances. Fortunately, Zephron (who had once been Zeus, the eldest Dreamer), was always able to help Waldo keep an even keel with his powerful mind.

Waldo sighed and gently moved Carlatta's arm away. He turned on his side and slowly quieted his mind. After a few minutes, he too was snoring.

CHAPTER 6

Test Inside Carlito's Mind

Carlos was laying on a medical gurney with several sensors attached to his head and torso. On the wall behind the gurney, a bank of medical equipment blinked with activity displaying Carlo's respiratory rate, blood pressure and other bodily functions

"What now?" he asked, looking at the others.

"Just let Zephron guide you and soon you'll go under," Waldo said.

Carlos closed his eyes and put his hands on his chest. Despite his courage and willingness to be the guinea pig for this experiment, Waldo could tell that his former grandson was tense.

Zephron Artemus stepped behind the gurney and put his hands on Carlos' head. The others in the room stood quietly as Zephron closed his eyes and moved his fingers around Carlos' skull. The professor's body stiffened somewhat, and Carlos' body relaxed. His hands fell to the side and went limp. After a few minutes the professor opened his eyes.

"He's under." Zephron whispered.

"Fine, now Om, Carlatta and I will link with you Zephron," Waldo began instructing in a soft voice. "Once we're linked, you will guide us all in. We'll enter through his Lower Mental Body and work our way into the Budhic Intuitive Plain. There, we'll have access to his subconscious and all the important elements of his personality. As I explained before, we're not to "address", "touch" or interact with any representations or images of Carlos when we're in there. Remember, we're not treating him. We're just acquainting ourselves with what it feels like to be inside an individual's mind. Zephron will be our "guide" and we are to listen and obey any and all instructions from him, is that clear?"

Om and Carlatta nodded in agreement.

"Fine let's begin," Waldo said, as he closed his eyes and grabbed Zephron's hand. The others followed suit by holding hands with Waldo.

The room they were in dissolved and Zephron, Waldo, Carlatta and Omega found themselves standing on the floor of a virtual representation of Mount Olympus. Behind Zephron and Omega, stood their old Dreamer bodies rising high into the forest's canopy. Behind Waldo and Carlatta, were their old Plantanimal bodies as Kelem and Animah. They looked at each other and smiled in remembrance of their old lives.

"It is good to be here again my friends," Waldo said.

"Indeed, but we cannot indulge ourselves now, we have a job to do," Zephron pointed out.

"What a shame," Carlatta added, feeling nostalgic for her days on Plantanimus.

"What next?" Omega asked.

"Look behind you." Zephron said, pointing to the image of a door that had materialized in the middle of the forest a few meters away. "That is our way in and out. I will enter first and guide you in. Once inside the first things you will see are representations of Carlo's thought forms. You will see many objects, some strange and some familiar. Many will be out of proportion. for example, you might see a child's toy the size of a building, or bizarre objects that seem to change form and shape. Pay no attention to any of these things, they have no mass or solidity. They are merely Carlo's ideas and concepts of reality on the physical plain. On the second level we will enter his Higher Mental Body, and here, we must proceed with some caution. This is where his creativity and intellect reside. Depending on his personality, it may seem a very chaotic and strange place or it might be very orderly and calm. We will huddle in a tight group until we reach his Budhic Intuitive

Plain where we can reside with complete safety," he paused and looked to the others. "Any questions?"

No one had any questions and they all followed Zephron as he headed toward the door.

Upon reaching the door, Zephron manifested a golden rope and unwinding it, he passed it to the others. "This is our safety line. As long as you hold on to it you will be fine. Just don't let go of it."

Zephron opened the door and entered first followed by Waldo, Carlatta and Omega bringing up the rear.

They soon found themselves in what appeared to be an open field of grass illuminated by an oversized sun. All about, were strewn thousands of objects, strange and familiar, as Zephron had told them they would find. Many were floating in the 'air'. Some floated so high in the 'sky' as to be barely visible. Many pieces were mechanical in shape and function, and Waldo recognized some to be the kind used in planet terraforming. Waldo smiled when the image of several beautiful women in various stages of undress drifted by the group off to one side. Carlatta saw them too and giggled like a little girl.

After a while, Zephron stopped and pointed to a hole in the surface of the "field" in front of them.

"This is the way to his Higher Mental Body. I don't know what it will feel like going in. We might experience a lack of "gravity" or feel like we're falling. In any case, don't panic and don't let go of the rope," he added, as he dropped into the opening followed by the others.

For a moment, Waldo thought of an ancient book called Alice In Wonderland as the group dropped into the 'rabbit's hole'. He held on tightly to the golden rope and reached back for Carlatta and held her hand tightly.

The sensation turned out to be more of a roller coaster ride along a tunnel brightly lit by long neon colored strands that pulsated on and off in a rhythmic beat. Soon, they had come out into what appeared to be the middle of outer space. All around could be seen thousands of stars and nebulae?... or things that appeared to be such objects in reality.

Waldo panicked briefly and held his breath, fearing instant decompression in the void of 'space'. "Remember, there is no air or lack of it in this place. You are not really here. Only the idea of you is here, and therefore, you cannot be affected by what you see or feel."

Waldo let go of his breath. "Thanks, Zephron. I needed to hear you say that."

"Me too!" echoed Carlatta, floating behind Waldo as she exhaled as well.

"We appear to be in the middle of outer space surrounded by stars and heavenly objects," interjected Omega, looking at the spectacle.

"I've seen this before in others back on Plantanimus when we were processing Pilgrims before the exodus. This kind of creative higher intellect "space void" is quite common amongst humans. I attribute it to ancient racial memories of early humanoid species' original experience of the cosmos," Zephron recalled.

"What next?" Waldo asked.

Zephron looked around and pointed to what appeared to be a gigantic Quasar shining brightly above them. "That is the entrance to Carlo's Budhic Intuitive Plain. Follow me." He floated upwards, dragging the others behind him.

As they rose in the near emptiness, the light from the object became brighter and brighter, it's light seemingly burning through the eyes of the foursome. "Remember, that this light is not real and no matter how bright or hot it may seem to you, it cannot harm us in any way," Zephron warned, anticipating what Waldo, Carlatta and Omega might be experiencing.

Their ascent gathered speed and it felt as though they were traveling at relativistic speed aimed at the center of the Quasar. Waldo, Carlatta and Omega held on to the golden rope for dear life. The sensation of speed became almost unbearable and then suddenly they all found themselves floating in a gently lit cloud, colored in soft pastels, surrounded by a warm physical sensation.

A large iridescent golden white column stood in the middle of this environment, leading up and down, its ends disappearing above and below in the floating mist.

"We've reached Carlo's Budhic Intuitive Plain. If we were to follow this shaft upwards which is called the Antahkarana," Zephron said, pointing up, "we would reach his Atmic Body or Plain, which is the seat of a person's spirituality. And if we were to go higher still, we would come to his Monadic Plain, which is where a person's true soul or higher self, resides. That is a person's highest state of being, which connects to the Universal Mind God, but still retains a sense of individuality. We won't be going any further "up" than here. And in any case, only Omega and I are skilled enough to reach the higher plains, and then, only when absolutely necessary, such as when we have to transmute a soul to a new body," he concluded.

Carlatta's eyes were opened wide in amazement. "It's beautiful Zephron," she said in wonder. "I had no idea that this experience would be so sacred and beautiful. I feel privileged to be here!"

"Quite so my dear, but then again, we're all just as wondrous in similar ways," Omega added.

"Look down," Zephron said, as the mist parted below them and the company of four could see the lower plains as individual universes attached to the Antahkarana like pearls on a string. "From the Budhic plain we can access an individual's lower Atmas or planes and gently correct any problems that might exist in a particular area. This is the extent of my skill and knowledge in these matters. When we enter Sulana's mind, we will have to rely on Waldo's previous experience and hope for the best."

"Thank you Zephron for guiding us here so skillfully and safely, we couldn't have done it without you, and now I feel confident that we'll be able to help Sulana without harming her," Waldo interjected.

"Very well then, let us depart from our dear friend Carlo's mind and return to our reality. There is much that we need to discuss before administering to Sulana. The way back will be much easier than the way in. From here we can "descend" through the Antahkarana directly back to our individual consciousness. Hold on to me. Here we go!"

Zephron disappeared into the golden shaft carrying Waldo, Carlatta and Omega with him. The inside of the column carried the four of them in a "downward" direction. The sensation was akin to passing through the birth canal but without any traumatic experience. The group suddenly exited through the door in the middle of the virtual forest in Plantanimus and found themselves standing in the same clearing where they had begun their journey. "You can let go of the chord," Zephron announced. And as he spoke the words, the golden rope dissolved into nothingness. Waldo, Carlatta and Omega smiled gratefully at Zephron for his skillful leadership and for bringing them back safely.

A second later, they were back in the room where Carlo's semiconscious body lay on the gurney. They let go of each other's hands and felt the need to shake their bodies.

"That was quite something," Waldo remarked, as he stretched his lanky frame.

"I feel as though I just came off a wild carnival ride," Carlatta added.

"You're experiencing a psychosomatic reaction to what your mind just went through. The moment you came back to yourself in this reality, the body made a physical adjustment to deal with the memory of the event," Zephron informed them, as he himself bent his torso sideways and exercised his arms.

"How long were we in…." Carlatta asked, wondering about the passage of time during their journey.

Waldo looked at his wrist comp and his eyebrows went up. "Why, it's only been a minute or two. I could have sworn that we were in there at least a half hour or longer!"

"The perception of time exists only on the Physical Plane, once you pass into the Astral Plane and then onto the Lower mental Body, time ceases to exist," commented Zephron.

"Now let's bring Carlos out of his meditative state," added Zephron, putting his handson Carlos' head once again. He closed his eyes, and a few moments later, both men opened their eyes simultaneously.

"I'm ready whenever you are," Carlos said, looking at the foursome standing around the gurney.

Waldo and Carlatta laughed at his comment.

"It's over Carlito, we're done!" Waldo said, smiling.

"Really, how long was I under? Carlos asked, confused.

"Only a few minutes Carlito, you did just fine. Thank you for volunteering. Your contribution will help us heal Sulana," added

Zephron, as he began disconnecting the various leads attached to Carlos' head.

Looking sheepish, Carlos asked, "You didn't find anything weird in there, did you guys?"

"Nothing out of the ordinary Carlito. As I've said before, you're the most mentally healthy person I've ever known," Waldo added, while patting his broad shoulders.

"Good to know!" Carlos said, jumping off the gurney. "You can call on me anytime you need to knock around my insides."

"Will do," said Zephron, smiling as well.

"Let's go back to the meeting room. We need to recount our experience and formulate a way to apply what we just learned to Sulana's case," Waldo suggested.

"Carlito, we don't need your assistance anymore, so you are free to go," Zephron informed Carlos.

"Fantastic, I think this experiment made me hungry, I'm heading for the kitchen to make myself a good meal! See you brainiacs later!" he added, as he jogged away from the treatment room.

After Carlos' exit the foursome also left the room and headed upstairs to the meeting room.

It was two dash seven in the afternoon, (about 5 pm Terran) when they all sat down at the oval table in the meeting room. The Centralian sun was now hovering just above the mountain range west of the mansion and would soon disappear below the snow covered peaks. The partially drawn red curtains gave the room a pleasing orange tint. Carlatta sat next to one of the windows and her long black hair showed hints of red under the sunlight. Waldo looked at her and imagined in his mind that a painter like Rembrandt would be inspired by her classic beauty and would want to paint a portrait of her just as she looked right now.

Carlatta caught his look and asked silently, mouthing the word. "What?"

Waldo leaned over and whispered in her ear. "Sometimes I get dizzy just looking at you!"

Carlatta's eyes shone brightly as she smiled happily at Waldo's complement.

Zephron and Omega noticed the exchange and smiled quietly. They were always pleased whenever the young couple expressed their undying love for each other. For Zephron who had re-birthed Waldo as Kelem and had created Carlatta as Anima centuries before, he felt the joy a parent feels for his own flesh and blood. For Omega, who had once been the youngest of the Dreamers, his happiness came from the feeling that Waldo and Carlatta were his beloved brother and sister.

Waldo shrugged somewhat self-consciously and looked at Zephron and Omega. "Sorry, I shouldn't be flirting with Carlatta at a moment like this," he said, with a serious expression.

"My dear boy," Omega interjected. "Your love for Carlatta serves to remind us of the beauty of the world. Nothing could be better than to remember such a fact, particularly at a moment like this!"

"Thank you for your kind words Om. The truth is, we're facing a big challenge with Sulana's condition and we need to come up with an approach that will succeed. I'm concerned with the fact that she is a Gulax, and as Zephron had mentioned before, we have no experience with her species. None of the pilgrims that came to Plantanimus seeking re-birth were Gulax, and so, we're in the dark as to what we can expect when we enter her mind."

"I've downloaded everything I could find from the inter-galactic data base regarding Gulax psychology," added Zephron. "From my research, I've found a few facts that will be helpful to us."

"Such as?" Omega inquired.

"Well, for one thing, the Gulax emotional life is expressed mainly through their intellect. And if their seven esoteric bodies don't resemble those of humanoids at all, it means that Sulana's Emotional Body (or Astral Plane), might not be in the same position along the Antahkarana as ours is."

Are you saying that Sulana's Higher Mental body and her Astral/Emotional Body might be one and the same?" asked Waldo, somewhat concerned.

"Precisely. And that means that her Higher Mental Plane's architecture could be radically different than ours," Zephron answered, with a worried expression. "As you all know, the Higher Mental Plane is where an individual's high intellect resides. In addition, I suspect that the Gulax intellect is more rigidly structured than a human's. In other words, more powerful than a humanoid in certain ways. It may also be so closely identified with the ego that it might be a place where aggression and primitive emotions all coexist with the intellect."

"And that could be dangerous," Omega mused, quietly.

"Yes," continued Zephron. "I suspect that when Sulana's memories of her life as Tarsia came forward in her mind, her Gulax Higher Mental Body shut down her physical body as a defense measure. It's possible that part of her psyche is barricaded behind a virtual defensive wall put up by her Intellectual/Emotional Body. It may be that she interprets the presence of Tarsia's personality as a threat."

"And to complicate matters," Omega added, expanding on Zephron's theory. "Tarsia herself was angry because of her temporary exile from Plantanimus. She was so traumatized by that event, that she wouldn't return to the family despite all our pleas over the years."

"Two personalities belonging to the same individual at war with each other, as in a person with multiple personality disorder," Waldo commented, almost as a question.

"Very similar in a way," Zephron agreed. "Known centuries ago, as Dissociative Identity Disorder or D.I.D. No cases have been known to occur for many centuries now, and it was believed to be caused partially by misplaced therapy or erroneous treatment. Many thought the disease to be merely a symptom of other mental illnesses and commonly misdiagnosed by psychiatrists. But for all intents and purposes, Sulana can be thought of as a D.I.D patient."

"How should we approach the problem then?" asked Waldo, suddenly feeling unsure.

"Before we bring her back to consciousness, Sulana's Higher Self must accept and recognize Tarsia as being part of her soul. That work might only be accomplished at the Monadic Plain level. In other words, her utmost highest self, residing just below the undifferentiated Universal Mind God. Her lower planes on the other hand, might present us with unnecessary risks," Zephron said pausing, as he searched for the right words. "I'm hesitant to enter an individual's highest point in their soul, merely to settle an argument that should be resolved in that individual's lower Mental Planes..." Zephron hesitated once again, this time looking far away, his face showing a deep conflict in his mind. "I don't know any other way to express what I'm thinking other than to say that by working with Sulana's lower planes, we all may be committing a grievous error."

Zephron's words surprised Omega, Waldo and Carlatta. They remained quiet for a spell and then Waldo spoke.

"I've never known you to be unsure when facing a challenge before my friend!" Waldo exclaimed with surprise. "Why not start in her Intellectual/Emotional Plane? What brings these doubts to your mind?"

"In spite of my accumulated knowledge, I must confess that dealing with a Gulax mind for the first time, is outside my realm of experience. I suppose that we must proceed anyway. We can't leave Sulana in her condition."

"Indeed," Omega agreed. "Perhaps we will be able to resolve her crisis without having to enter her Monadic Plane. Zephron, I think that your hesitation to work in her Intellectual/Emotional Plane has more to do with your concern for Waldo and Carlatta's safety."

Zephron appeared chagrined at Omega's accurate statement regarding his concern for the young couple. Waldo's face lit up recognizing that his old friend Zeus was not suddenly filled with doubt but afraid for him and Carlatta.

"My dear Zephron," Waldo began saying, with relief in his voice. "We've all been through so much together over the centuries, and we've faced big and scary foes in the past. I love the fact that you're so protective of Carlatta and me, but please remember that despite our youthful appearance, my beloved and I have lived more than six hundred years. We may be mere children chronologically, but we're more than capable of holding our own."

"Forgive me Waldo. Being in a human body does have its drawbacks. These are the only times when I wish I was still a Dreamer, immune to chemically induced emotions from my human brain," Zephron confessed to Waldo and Carlatta with a smile.

"There's nothing to forgive Zephron. I feel certain that Sulana's therapy must take place in her Higher Mental Body as you've already ascertained, regardless of whether her Emotional body resides there as well. We'll figure out a way to keep ourselves safe, and I know that we'll succeed with the protection of your powerful mind."

"It's agreed then," Omega stated. "We have a strategy and now we only need to work on the finer details of our mission. But first, what say you we break for dinner and feed these human bodies before we all faint!"

"You're right, let's eat dinner and reconvene here to iron out our plan." Zephron agreed and looked at the others. "I think that we should begin Sulana's treatment at midnight. Does that sound right to all of you?"

"Midnight sounds good, let's go eat!" Waldo said, as they all stood up from their chairs and left the room.

The sun now but a thin disk floating above the mountains behind the mansion, blinked and dove below the edge of the highest peak. The room's color changed from a deep orange to a deep blue.

CHAPTER 7

Dinner and a Meditation

Susan and Terence sat by a large window surrounded by boxes of household supplies. They were in a utility room in the attic that faced the front of the mansion. The two of them always came here when they wanted to get away from the hustle and bustle of the house. They had formed a strong bond in this incarnation and each usually sought the other when things were difficult. This was one of those times. The hour was late, and the sun was waning to the west. From the window they could see the town's artificial lights coming on here and there, as day turned to night in the valley below.

They were twenty years apart chronologically and unrelated by blood, but once, they had been brother and sister back on Plantanimus with only three years between them. As Gutan the oldest sibling, and she as Animahali, the oldest of the Rogeston girls, they had lived together on Earth while Dario, the second oldest brother had resided there as well. Being the oldest, they were the first three siblings to be sent away from Plantanimus and had always felt closer to each other than to the rest of the Rogeston children. Susan was very concerned about Thula and had asked Terence to meet her here to talk to him about the current situation regarding Sulana.

"Is she resting comfortably now?" Terence was saying.

"Yes. Om has been quieting her mind to keep her calm but she's so sad now Ter, it breaks my heart!"

Terence's eyes reflected his own heartbreak and he reached for Susan's hand. "I never understood her obsession with Tarsia. And as much as I loved Tarsia then and now, why are we as a family so bent on keeping the ten Rogeston kids together even after four centuries have passed?"

"We're unusual Ter you know that! Even though we are now birthed by other bloodlines, we have to remain together to continue the work we've been doing all along."

Terence looked at the town below and sighed, his face showing frustration. "Maybe Tarsia was right in leaving and never coming back. After all, we've gotten along well without her presence all this time."

"Please Ter, don't say that! She's one of us and she's been a lost soul for all these years, and no matter how Thula may have worsened the situation right now, I for one, am glad that we have a chance to reunite with our long-lost sister."

"That may not be possible considering what's happened to Sulana," Terence commented, wryly. "I hope Zephron, Om and Waldo know what they're doing!"

"Are you upset because they didn't include you in their attempt to treat Sulana?"

"No, not at all Susan! My work has always been more theoretical than practical and I would have turned them down if they had asked me anyway. "I'm just not sure that they'll be able to succeed in their attempt because of Sulana being a Gulax."

"You really think that her being a Gulax presents such a problem?"

"I don't know, I don't know!" Terence said, with exasperation. "To be honest with you, I'm more concerned about Thula right now. As a matter of fact, I've been worried about her for a very long time now."

Susan had known about Terence's concern for their youngest sister over the years. But now, he seemed angry, and even desperate about her condition. "Ter, you're scaring me. What's going on with you?"

"From the very beginning and through subsequent incarnations, Thula has always been the Rogeston's beast of burden when it came to solving our problems. Always getting us out of trouble and taking on responsibility! Is it any wonder that she's suddenly having real problems in this life? And I know that Grandfather..., I mean Waldo, says that she'll pull out of this awkward stage that she's going through now. But I tell you Susan, I've seen her struggle more each time that she's re-born." Terence paused for a moment, his breathing had quickened, and his face was flushed. "Maybe we should send her away and tell her to go and have whatever kind of life she wants to have. Let her have a "vacation life" for once this time," he added, then began pacing the length of the room.

"You don't mean that do you, Ter?" asked Susan, her eyes following him as he walked back and forth.

Terence stopped and sat by the window, pulling his legs up to his chest. He was quiet for a moment and then he turned to Susan with a quizzical look in his eyes. "Haven't you wondered why Thula has not had any of her own children since the exodus from Plantanimus? And doesn't it bother you that she's only been a mother once and that it's been more than three hundred years since she had any children of her own?

"I've thought about it on and off over the years Ter. But I must say, it's not that unusual for some of us to choose bachelorhood during certain incarnations. I'm nearly forty now and I doubt that I'll have children in this life."

"Yes, but you've been a mother three times since then, and Thula has not borne any children since 2856!"

Susan fell quiet and looked at Terence. She didn't have a quick answer to his challenge.

Terence shook his head and looked out the window. Night had fallen by now and the darkness seemed to match his mood.

"It was one thing for her to create the technology to give us all new bodies back then. But I think that the nullification of the Tau Fortresses put a scar in her spirit that hasn't healed to this day."

"But Terence, she recovered well from that effort during her life as Tatiana. I've never seen any long lasting effects from that experience in her personality."

Terence let out a short sarcastic laugh when he heard Susan's words. "Haven't you? I have! Knowing her altruistic nature I think she felt she needed to hide her condition from all of us. And she hid it quite expertly even from someone like me, who was already knowledgeable in the workings of the mind. After she destroyed the fortresses, I remember seeing her struggle with little mundane things for the rest of her natural life as Tatiana. And during her next life, she suffered from nightmares until she was a teenager. I know, because we were both the same age then. You were already an adult during that period, so you missed a lot of things about her back then. After that, I've noticed a decline in her ability to deal with stress and difficult situations. In lifetime after lifetime Thula seems less and less able to face adversity."

Terence's words had darkened Susan's mood as well. But she refused to think so negatively and hopelessly as he was now.

"I love you Ter, but you always tend to see the negative side of things. I agree with you that there might be some lingering after-effects from Tatiana's mighty struggle with the Tau Fortresses on Plantanimus, but I think that Thula's current problems stem more from some sort of temporary chemical imbalance in her young brain. After all, she's only seventeen! And besides, you know very well that each new body we're born into, changes us in significant ways."

"That's true Susan. But as I've said before, she's been declining little by little with each incarnation." Terence's face became somber. "Maybe we're not supposed to keep coming back from life to life."

Susan smiled, trying to appear upbeat. She was sensing his deep despair and doom and it was beginning to affect her mood.

"We always have a choice Ter," she said affectionately, holding his hand in a motherly way. "Alexei and Kani gave up the ghost after one life, refusing to be put in new bodies. Our parents were at peace when they passed on."

Terence sighed. "They were very special, unusual people alright! Lately, I've been feeling that I might call it quits after this life. I've accomplished enough in all my lifetimes. And look at Faruk! How he struggles in old age like he is now. What is he now, ninety-nine, a hundred? He doesn't die well. And yet, he keeps coming back. I think having the choice to come back is a trap of sorts. After all, it's very hard to give up the choice to live again!"

"You'll be reincarnated anyway Ter, except that you'll be reborn outside of the family so why not come back?"

"I know I'm sure to come back, but at least it will be through a natural process and not through the auspices of the Rogeston Clan," Terence responded, sourly.

They both sat quietly for a while reflecting on all that had been said. Susan broke the silence first.

"Listen Ter, I understand how you feel, but I think that we should be talking about Thula and Sulana and how we can help them now."

Terence nodded and rested his chin on his hands. "You're right. Here I am going on and on about how bad I feel, meanwhile our two sisters are suffering through a terrible crisis. What can we do Susan? How can we help them?"

"Well, Sulana is being looked after by Waldo, Zephron, Om and Carlatta. We should concentrate on Thula and see if we can raise her mood while all this other stuff is going on. We have to make her feel better and strengthen her spirit. Heaven forbid if things don't go well with Sulana. Thula's going to need all the help she can get."

"You're right sister," Terence said, smiling now. "What would I do without your positive spirit and encouragement routinely lifting me out of the doldrums?"

"Oh, I don't know. You'd probably sink into a dark pit of hopeless despair and shrivel like a dead weed!"

Terence laughed, his mood improving a little by her sarcastic joke. Terence was glad that Susan knew him better perhaps than even he knew himself. He smiled and then reached for his sister and gave her a warm hug. Susan was glad to see Terence in a better mood, but her attempt to lift his spirits had taken a toll on her. As she sat there hugging him, she had to fight to keep tears from her eyes.

She pulled away from his arms and looked at him with a smile. "Let's go and give Thula what she needs."

"You're right!" Terence answered, taking Susan's hand as they left the attic. When they reached her room, they found that she wasn't there. A colony member that helped keep the mansion clean, came by and told them that she'd seen Carlos and Thula head downstairs.

"If I know Carlos, he's down in the kitchen cooking and eating something!" Terence said lightly as they took to the stairs.

When they reached the kitchen, they did indeed find Carlos cooking something in a big frying pan next to Thula who was chopping vegetables on the center island.

"Hey you two!" Susan said cheerfully. "What's for dinner?"

They both turned their heads toward the door and Thula made a good attempt at looking happy. Her smile looked pasted in but at least she was trying.

"I'm making Carlito's famous spicy fish. Thula here, is making Ratatouille," Carlos added, with typical humor.

"We're making dinner for everybody. The others will be down shortly," Thula said, returning to her chopping duties.

"Hmmm, smells heavenly Carlito," Susan said. "I think you missed your calling, you should have been a chef instead of a terraformer."

"Cooking and terraforming are very similar. Both involve chemistry, physics, artistry, talent and of course it doesn't hurt to be dashingly handsome to boot," Carlos commented with a serious expression.

"It's a miracle that we can all fit here in the kitchen with the size of your ego and all," Susan said, as she walked in and went to the counter where she opened up a drawer and took out silverware to help set the big table in the center of the room.

In response, Carlos laughed. Terence rolled his eyes comically as he went over to help Thula with the vegetables.

"How are you feeling little one?" he asked tenderly.

"I'm alright." Thula answered quietly, not taking her eyes off her vegetables.

"That's good. Everything's going to be alright Thula, don't you worry your young head about nothing."

"Thanks Ter, you're really sweet. When I heard about Carlito volunteering to be a guinea pig for the others, I realized I was being a baby feeling sorry for myself and all."

"That's wonderful Thula. Although I think Carlito wanted the others in his head so that they could fix whatever's wrong with him," Terence said out loud, so that Carlos could hear him.

"Jealousy, pure jealousy Thula. I'm telling you, these two can't stand my wonderfulness!" Carlos shot back sticking out his tongue at Susan and Terence as he continued frying fish.

Thula's face lit up with a genuine smile hearing the witty repartee.

Terence and Susan glanced at each other with hope in their eyes. Perhaps Thula's state of mind wasn't so bad after all. The upstairs door leading down to the kitchen from the main floor opened and Waldo yelled. "Hey down there! When is dinner going to be ready? We're starving up here!"

"Patience Waldo. It should be about ten minutes or so!" Shouted Carlos from the stove.

"Mmm, it smells wonderful Carlito. I'm always glad whenever you're in the house. You're cooking is superb!"

"Finally, somebody acknowledges my genius!" Carlos pronounced triumphantly.

"Please Waldo, don't encourage the man. It's difficult enough dealing with his overbearing personality as it is!" yelled Susan, from the dining table.

Waldo's laughter could be heard as he closed the door. Carlos began whistling a silly melody as he continued working his cuisine magic.

To an uninformed witness, the scene in the kitchen would have appeared to them as the normal everyday activity of a close-knit family. Beneath everyone's casual behavior however, lay an unspoken tension that everyone was trying very hard to hide.

No matter what was being said and how everyone was acting, everyone in the house knew that the next few hours would be crucial to the wellbeing of two of their own. From Zephron on down, every member of the Rogeston clan was using their powerful psychic abilities to raise Thula's spiritual vibrations, and at the same time, preparing themselves for the attempt to rescue Sulana Kay's mind from her accidental self-induced psychic coma.

Later that night around three dash eight, Omega took Thula up to her room and helped her enter a very deep meditative state. Soon, she was asleep soundly and would remain so until late morning. Omega knew that the attempt to rescue Sulana from her condition was going to require the full attention of the entire colony, and especially, the talent and abilities of Zephron, Waldo, Carlatta and himself. They needed to focus their minds on the task ahead.

He closed the door to Thula's room quietly and headed for the reception hall downstairs at the front of the mansion. About a hundred members of the colony were assembling to participate in a group meditation to help the foursome prepare for the difficult task ahead. As he reached the main floor, he ran into some of the faculty members of the college. He said a casual hello to several of them and hurried on to the reception hall.

When he reached the main atrium at the front of the mansion, he recognized several members of the original Plantanimus colony milling around, engaged in conversation as they waited for the meditation to begin.

A few of them were original Dreamers now in human bodies. He reflected on how most of the formal Dreamers had chosen to remain closely knit with each other and to Zephron and Waldo since the exodus from Plantanimus. Only he, Omega, Zephron and ten others had individuated themselves sufficiently to be able to stay away from the main group of about seven hundred and eighty-four ex-Dreamers, for years at a time. Most of them were still processing their individuality as a 'soul group'. It would be another century or two before they all would begin to develop their higher bodies to the point where they would see themselves as true individuals.

Omega had been the youngest of the Dreamers and had achieved sentience last of all. Yet, because his "body" was situated closest to Kelem and Anima's cottage on Plantanimus, he had had more contact with all the Rogestons than most of the other Dreamers. Mostly with the children, who literally grew up around him and considered him a 'friend' throughout their childhood.

Though he never confessed it to anyone, not even Zephron, Tatiana had always been his favorite among the children. When she began to transfer the Dreamer's consciousness into human bodies, Omega was the second dreamer to receive his human body after Zeus. In many ways, he always saw Tatiana/Thula as his sister.

Waldo, Susan and Terence were standing by the entrance to the reception hall talking to a few members of the colony and when they saw him, they motioned at him to come to them.

"How is Thula?" Waldo asked.

"She's fine. I put her into a deep trance and she's sure to sleep soundly until mid-morning," Omega answered.

Terence reached for Omega's shoulder and thanked him for taking care of Thula. "Thanks Om. We really appreciate your expert hand in this."

"We owe her a great deal, Ter. She's going to be fine, you'll see," Omega replied, patting Terence's hand.

Susan, who had been answering a question from one of the colonists, turned her attention to the group and joined the conversation. "I heard you say that she's alright, Om. Thank heavens!" she said.

"Are you ready?" Waldo asked the other three. "I think we should start the meditation."

"Yes, let's start now", agreed Terence. "It's three dash ten and if we group-meditate for about an hour we should be able to start with Sulana a little past midnight.

Waldo nodded. Then he moved to the center of the atrium and raised his voice. "Attention friends. Let's all assemble in the reception room. We're about to begin."

The conversation ceased immediately and the crowd obediently filed into the reception room quietly. Despite his boyish looks, Waldo was still Kelem to everyone and his word was law. Everyone in the colony down to the last man woman and child, held the utmost admiration for Waldo and would not hesitate to give up his or her life for the man who they considered to be their beloved and respected leader.

As was the custom, two very large and muscular young men from the colony stood guard by the exquisitely carved double doors to the reception hall, acting as sergeant at arms, ensuring that the group would not be interrupted and disturbed while they meditated. As soon as the last person entered the room, they closed the massive doors and stood guard.

Inside, Waldo lowered the lights and Zephron began speaking in a soft voice guiding the group into a deep state of meditation. In a few minutes, the entire company had joined their minds as one and begun raising the group's spiritual vibrations to clear any negative energies from the mansion. Their main mission was to supply the foursome with massive amounts of mental energy to help heal Sulana Kay. She had once been Tarsia Rogeston, daughter of Alexei and Kani, and granddaughter of Kelem and Anima. A lost soul who had returned to the fold, after many, many years.

CHAPTER 8

Sulana Accepts Tarsia

Sulana lay on an operating table on the stage of the mansion's oval shaped medical amphitheater, her hands and feet bound by strong restrains to prevent her from harming herself or others. Gulax claws are extremely sharp and their strength was legendary. Even a thin wiry "lizard" such as Sulana could potentially tear deep gashes in the flesh of anyone near her during the procedure.

Several nano leads were attached to her body connected to a battery of electronic equipment monitoring all her bodily functions. Only Waldo, Zephron, Omega, Carlatta and three medical technicians were present. The rest of the colony had retired to their homes and apartments and would remain still and quiet until it was announced that Sulana's procedure was done. Many would remain in deep prayer, communicating with the All Mighty Universal Mind God asking for the successful conclusion of the attempt to bring Sulana back to health.

Waldo, Carlatta and Zephron stood by the table waiting for Omega, who was performing last minute checks of all the equipment and was giving final instructions to the three young technicians who would be assisting. In his previous incarnation, Omega had been a physician and even though he had chosen a different career path in this life, the group usually relied on him when it came to serious issues of health.

Omega came to the table and joined the group, carrying with him four metal bracelets attached to a silver metallic box via thin wires.

He placed the box on the table and clipped one of the bracelets on his wrist and then handed one to each of the other three members of the group. "We're ready to start." he began saying and then pointing to the devices as he handed them out, he continued. "These are sensing devices that we usually put on patients during surgery. However, I've reprogrammed them to act as a safety device should we run into any problems. Basically, if any of us begin showing signs of physical distress during the procedure, the bracelets will give a mild electric shock to the body which will bring the individual or all of us back to reality should the need arise."

"Thank you, Om. We appreciate any advantage that we can get in this circumstance," Zephron said.

"Still, we must rely on our wits and Zephron's powerful mind as well," Waldo added.

"Relax everyone," Carlatta said sweetly. "Everything's going to be fine. I know we're going to succeed."

The three men nodded and smiled, glad to hear the female in the group being so positive and reassuring. Omega turned to one of the technicians and signaled for the lights to be brought down low.

Once again, Zephron was at the head of the table and he put his hands on Sulana's head as he had done earlier today with Carlos. He closed his eyes and remained there for a while. The others could see Zephron's eyes moving back and forth looking like someone dreaming in the midst of a REM cycle. After a while, he opened his eyes and looked at the others with concern. "It looks as though she's barricaded herself behind a virtual defensive wall of desert thorn bushes. The environment looks to be a scene from the Tak Desert on Gulax Prime."

The others exchanged glances somewhat confused. "I thought Sulana was born and raised on Terra Prime. It's strange that in her mind she's retreated to a virtual version of the Gulax desert," Waldo commented.

"It might be a species-specific racial memory," Zephron said pensively. "And then again it's quite possible that as a child, her parents taught her through stories and anecdotes about the Gulax home world and about the customs and history of their species."

"Hmmm, I see," Waldo mused. "To an impressionable young Gulax, learning about her heritage could have imprinted on her the idea that the home world was a place of safety and comfort in spite of her experiences growing up on Earth."

"This could mean that she might have regressed to a feral state of behavior and would feel threatened by anyone invading her space," Zephron added.

"How should we proceed?" Carlatta asked, looking at Zephron, sensing the threat of imminent danger hanging in the air.

Zephron rubbed his chin and was quiet for a moment. Then he looked up and stared at Waldo and Carlatta with an intense look in his eyes.

"If I remember correctly, as Tarsia, Sulana left Plantanimus very angry with her parents and blamed them for abandoning her to exile. But I seem to recall that she never assigned any responsibility to the two of you in that regard is that correct?" Zephron concluded, looking at Waldo and Carlatta.

Waldo and Carlatta looked at each other for a moment and they both nodded in assent.

Zephron remained pensive and looked down again considering a safe approach to the problem. After a while, he looked up again. This time with a smile in his face.

"You two should appear to her as Kelem and Anima in your Plantanimal bodies. The sight of you both as her grandparents is sure to evoke a positive response from Sulana and make it easier for me and Omega to work unseen. In other words, we'll both be there with you, but we'll be invisible to her. This way we'll minimize any possible aggressive reaction from her."

"I so miss those days back on Plantanimus," Carlatta said wistfully. "Yes, I would love to be Anima once again if only for a little while."

"And slipping on Kelem's personality will be like putting on a comfortable shirt and a pair of old pants. They may be old but after so many years the fabric has shaped itself to my body," Waldo concluded with a smile.

"Perfect. Let's proceed then," Omega said.

The four of them joined hands and closed their eyes.

The hum and beeps emitted by the monitoring equipment slowly faded away in their ears as the foursome transitioned to a deep state of meditation. They soon found themselves on a small depression in the middle of a large plain in the Gulaxian desert. Waldo and Anima's eyes squinted in reaction to the virtual brightness of the sun. Even though they knew that they weren't there physically, the sensation of extreme heat assailed their senses, nonetheless. Unlike Mars, the Gulaxian desert was truly red. Gulax Prime was replete with iron ore. The surface sedimentary rocks that formed the top soil of the planet billions of years before were 21 % iron ore mixed with other iron ore-bearing minerals such as smectite, hematite maghemite, magnetite as well as high sulfur and chlorine content. Gulax Prime was a harsh environment perfectly suited for the physiology of the Gulax. Their reptilian skin was immune to the powerful ultra violet rays of their sun and resistant to the acidic content of the atmosphere.

A strong gust of wind swept past them carrying the smell of dried vegetation from somewhere nearby. The wind swirled and turned into dust devils spinning like miniature tornados picking up dusty red sand and small pebbles in the superheated air carrying them away. To the uneducated observer this place looked completely real.

About a hundred meters away, a single outcrop of large brownish red boulders could be seen on the edge of the depression as the terrain rose to meet the arid plain. Surrounded by bizarre large yellow plants looking like a cross between trees and spiny cacti, the spot appeared to be the only place in the immediate area that could afford any shade or shelter.

Waldo and Carlatta heard Zephron's voice in their heads. "That's where Sulana is, she's barricaded herself with a wall of dead branches from those yellow thorny trees. There is a small cove inside that group of boulders. The place is a cul-de-sac and she's placed herself against the farthest wall from the entrance."

"It sounds as if she's expecting an attack," Waldo said, looking at the group of boulders in the distance.

"She appears to be in a state of panic. She seems agitated and in fear of her life," Zephron commented.

Carlatta reached out for Waldo and held his arm. "She's probably really scared and confused. We must reassure her that we're here to help her."

Waldo caressed her face affectionately. "We will my beloved. We must be very gentle and soft spoken with her so as not to alarm her. Perhaps you should be the first one to approach her. I'm sure that a female will seem less threatening to her in her current state of mind."

"Of course, my love. But how should I go about it? Do you have any suggestions?" asked Carlatta.

"When you reach the entrance to the cul-de-sac you should announce yourself as Anima, her grandmother and ask for permission to enter her 'space'," Zephron's disembodied voice said in Carlatta's head.

Waldo and Carlatta started walking toward the large boulders and when they reached them they slowed down. Waldo stayed slightly behind so as to not be 'seen' by Sulana when Carlatta showed herself at the entrance to the U-shaped cul-de-sac.

Carlatta turned back and gave Waldo a passionate kiss and then they held each other for a while looking at each other tenderly. Waldo couldn't help but be amazed at the realistic feel of Carlatta in Plantanimal form as Anima. Her green eyes and skin looked so true to the being that he knew for over three hundred years as his soul mate. A deep longing for that idyllic past that they had once enjoyed on Plantanimus struck his heart with a great feeling of nostalgia. Without saying it, he knew that Carlatta was feeling the same way.

Zephron's voice suddenly interrupted their idyll. "C'mon you two! Now's not the time to dwell in the past," he said with some humor.

They both smiled sheepishly and Carlatta broke away from Waldo's arms and slowly made her way back to the entrance.

Carlatta centered herself and spoke out loud in a gentle tone of voice. "Sulana it's me Anima, I want to talk to you my child. Can I come in?"

The response was only the sound of the wind.

Carlatta repeated her question, hoping for an answer this time.

A reptilian hiss issued forth from within the walls of the Cul-de-sac.

"I know you're scared my darling, but I mean you no harm. I just want to talk to you. Please don't be afraid of me."

"Go away, go away!" came back Sulana's response from the rear of the u-shaped enclosure. Her voice was pitched high and sounded hysterical.

"Please Sulana, don't send me away child. I want to help you. I know that you're very upset and I'm here for you."

Sulana began whimpering. Her crying echoing back and forth inside the rock formation. "What's happening to me?" she croaked in between sobs. "I don't understand what's happening to me."

"Let me in my child. I can help you understand what's happening to you," Carlatta added, her voice near the breaking point.

"Careful Carlatta don't give in to emotionalism. You must remain detached from her suffering. Otherwise you could get trapped in her turmoil," Zephron's voice warned.

"I'm not your child! Why do you keep calling me that?" Sulana yelled back.

Carlatta composed herself and continued. "Because you are my child, at least part of you is. Search your mind and you'll remember that once I held you in my arms as a little baby, a long time ago."

"That's insane you're a human not a lizard. You're trying to trick me!" Sulana responded.

Carlatta stepped into the entrance making sure that she was in Sulana's line of sight and showed herself as Anima.

"I'm not human Sulana, as you can plainly see," Carlatta said, her arms spread apart showing that she wasn't armed.

"Who are you?" came Sulana's response, upon seeing the image of Anima at the entrance to the cul-de-sac.

"I've told you, I'm Anima, your grandmother."

Sulana hissed and spat at Carlatta from her hiding place. "Anima's dead. She's been dead for a long time, you're an impostor!"

"Then who am I?" Carlatta asked.

"Well you look like her and sound like her, but you couldn't be her. Anima died when the Dreamers died," Sulana argued logically, though her tone showed signs of confusion.

"How is it that you know I sound like her?" Carlatta challenged Sulana. "Only someone that has heard Anima's voice could say that I sound like her. No one outside of Plantanimus has ever heard Anima speak."

This gave Sulana pause and Carlatta and the others hoped that she was mulling this fact in her mind. This was a good sign. Perhaps, she was beginning to remember her identity as Tarsia.

"Come closer," Sulana said, with tension in her voice.

Carlatta stepped inside the boundaries of the rock formation, and slowly walked toward the rear of the rock wall where Sulana had gathered her defensive wall of spiny branches.

"That's far enough," she said tensely. "Sit on that rock on your right," she ordered.

Carlatta obeyed and sat down where Sulana had indicated.

After a while, Sulana stirred behind her wall of thorns and Carlatta could see the outline of her body as she came near the front of her barricade and peered at her through a small opening between branches. Her yellow reptilian eyes regarded Anima's physical form carefully. After a while, she looked to the side as if remembering something, and then turned her gaze back Carlatta.

"You said you held me in your arms as a baby. I don't remember that," Sulana said dryly,never taking her eyes off Anima's form. She still seemed suspicious of Carlatta. However, there was curiosity in her voice.

"I don't suppose you remember that part so easily. After all, you were somebody else when I held you as an infant."

"What do you mean somebody else? Who was I?"

"Your name was Tarsia and you knew me as your grandmother."

"I never met my grandmother. She was dead by the time I was born. Besides, I'm Gulax and you're a..." Sulana hesitated for a moment, seemingly confused. "You're a Plantanimal, you couldn't be my grandmother. You're the wrong species!" Sulana concluded, with a sarcastic hiss/laugh.

"Ah yes, but you were not a Gulax when you were Tarsia. You were half human half Tarsian then. You were named after your birth mother's home world."

"You're talking about Kani Rogeston, aren't you? You're saying that she was my mother then. You're saying that I'm Tarsia Rogeston her daughter!" Sulana hissed/laughed loudly now and then backed against the rock behind her. Her voice changing suddenly and sounding paranoid again. "Hah, that's funny because I have Tarsia prisoner back here. What do you think of that! I have her all tied up bound and gagged, that's what I did!" she continued hissing/laughing, mocking Carlatta. "You're a dammed liar is what you are, what do you think of that!" she finished, sounding proud of herself.

"Careful Carlatta, when you mentioned Kani she became angry. She obviously still feels that her parents betrayed her, so try to avoid talking about them and concentrate on your past relationship with her as Anima." Zephron interjected.

"You must release Tarsia immediately, Sulana. She's a part of you. By holding her prisoner you're locking part of yourself as well," Carlatta continued.

Sulana remained quiet.

Carlatta centered herself once again and thought hard about what to say next.

"When you were about three years old back on Plantanimus, you started going to the Dreamer forest just outside our cottage and played around Omega's trunk, do you remember that?" Carlatta asked sweetly. "And every year after that, on the eve of the winter solstice, you and the whole family would gather around Omega's trunk around midnight and wait for the night blooming orchids around his roots to bloom."

Carlatta paused and was encouraged when Sulana came back to the front of her wall of thorns. She peered at Carlatta once again with curiosity in her eyes.

"I remember that. Continue," she said.

"Well if you remember that, you'll also remember that because of Omega's night blooming orchids you became interested in botany and biology. Something that you loved and is what you decided to study as a career," Carlatta added.

Sulana began to cry again, this time softly and sorrowfully sounding like a young girl. "I loved sitting next to Omega and talking to him about plants and how the Dreamers had made all the vegetation on Plantanimus. He talked to me in my head and showed me how Zeus and the others made all the flowers and fruit trees. And when mom and dad sent me away, I didn't want to leave and I cried for a long time because I missed everybody and specially Om, who was my dear friend," Sulana leaned back against the rock wall and slowly slid down to the floor to a sitting position, and continued crying.

"Would you like to talk to Omega, Sulana?" Carlatta asked, hoping that she would say yes.

"He's here, how can that be?" Sulana asked with surprise.

"Yes, he's here and he very much would like to talk to you again. But you should know that he's no longer a Dreamer. He's in a different body now and is living as a human. Would you allow him to talk to you?"

"Did Tatiana change him to a human? Why did she do that? Did it hurt when she did that to him?" Sulana asked, concerned for the welfare of her old friend.

"No, it didn't hurt him at all Sulana. And furthermore, if Tatiana hadn't changed him to a human, Omega would have died."

"Where is he? I want to see him! Can he come over here now?

"Yes. Will you allow him to come in here so that you can see him?" Carlatta asked.

"Yes, yes! I want to talk to him right away!"

"Well old friend, it appears that you must become visible now," Zephron said to Omega telepathically. "I suggest you make your voice sound exactly like it sounded to Tarsia when you were a Dreamer."

Omega's body "materialized" just outside the cul-de-sac and he entered and stopped when he reached the rock where Carlatta was sitting. Carlatta stood up and walked away.

Omega sat down on the rock and smiled at Sulana. "How are you Tarry? It's been so long since we talked," Omega said, using his old voice and calling her by her childhood nickname.

"Oh, it is you!" Sulana said, now coming back to the wall of thorns. "I never thought I would see or hear from you again. And here you are after all these years!"

"I missed you as well. Why didn't you come back to us little one? Remember the day you left Plantanimus? How you swore you'd come back as soon as you could? What happened to you? What kept you away?"

Sulana stood up and began tearing apart the wall forcefully. Zephron, Waldo and Carlatta became alarmed, fearing that Sulana was going to attack Omega. But he held them back, sensing that this was not an act of aggression but an emotional breakthrough, "Hold on," he told the others. "I think she wants to come to me."

The others held their virtual "breath" until they heard Omega talking calmly to Sulana.

Sulana walked over to Omega and sank to her knees in front of her old friend and embraced him, crying tears of relief. She told him the story of her former life and how for over six hundred years Tarsia's soul, now living in Sulana's body had been held prisoner in a limbo created by her own lower self, due to her inability to deal with the cruelty of the world outside of Plantanimus.

Her sensitive nature had been unable to withstand the negativity and insensitive behavior of others, and her life on Tarsia Prime had been marred by the prejudice and disdain of many naturally born Tarsians who considered her an inferior half-breed. She couldn't understand how her own family could have sent her away, abandoning her to such a ruinous fate.

Eventually, she turned inwards and withdrew from reality, and as time went by, she fell victim to insanity and was admitted to a Tarsian mental hospital. The facility discovered her identity and was about to contact the Rogeston family as to her whereabouts, when she escaped from the hospital. Afraid to be sued by the powerful and well known Rogeston family, the facility erased any records of her admittance and hid the truth from the world. Somehow, she managed to get hired as a crew member on a Kuralian freighter bound for the 'outlands', which was then the fringes of the known galaxy, and left Tarsia Prime never to return. After that, her life became a series of bad experiences leading her down an unlucky path of physical abuse by others, drug addiction and eventual death in an unmarked grave. She felt guilty that she had left the family behind and had lived such a poor life and blamed herself for her weakness and the pain she caused her family.

All this she told Omega as he soothed her and comforted her reassuring her that she was still beloved by the family, all the Dreamers, and the rest of the Plantanimus Colony.

During this process her physical appearance kept changing from Sulana to Tarsia and back. She was confused and asked him to help her understand what her real identity was.

Omega felt out of his element in this matter, and called for Zephron, Waldo and Carlatta to come and assist him in this task.

"Tarry, I think that your grandparents Kelem and Anima and Zeus can answer these questions better than I can. May call them and ask them to come here and sit with us?"

She agreed. Then, Waldo, Zephron and Carlatta walked into the cul-de-sac and greeted Sulana, each taking a turn holding her tightly in a warm embrace. Zephron explained to Sulana that he too had taken on human form and she accepted him as such.

They all sat around cross legged on the ground. Waldo spoke first. "Tarry, just as you no longer have the same body that your soul once imbued with life as Tarsia, neither do the three of us exist in our old forms as Kelem, Anima and Zeus. Do you understand?"

"You mean grandma and grandpa don't look like Plantanimals anymore?" she said, pointing to Waldo and Carlatta.

"Well," Zephron began "Omega and I look exactly like you see us now. As a matter of fact, you've already seen us both in our real bodies, except that you don't remember right now. But both your grandparents live now in human bodies as well."

Sulana looked at Waldo and Carlatta quizzically. Her personality as Tarsia temporarily overshadowing the Sulana identity.

"You've seen me as a blonde young man named Waldo. Here, let me show you," he said, pausing and reforming his image as Waldo.

Sulana was startled and she instinctively pulled back a little.

"Don't be afraid, I'm still Kelem your grandfather. Except that now I've reincarnated into a new body."

Sulana accepted that fact and then turned to Carlatta. "What about you grandma? What do you look like now?"

"I also look different. But I'm not going to show you my current form until later," Carlatta told her. "It would only confuse matters at this point. What's important my love, is that you let the other girl named Sulana stay "awake" in her body, which is the body that she's living in right now, do you understand?"

"This is not my body?" Sulana asked, looking at her physical form which had switched to Tarsia once again.

"No, my dear. You no longer have that body. That physical form disintegrated when you passed on many years ago. Remember what you just told Omega about your life story as Tarsia?" Waldo asked her.

"Yes, of course I remember. But I'm confused as to what you want me to do now!" Tarsia's personality said, feeling a little frustrated.

The foursome exchanged glances knowing that this was a delicate point in the process. Tarsia's personality had re-emerged and had come out of her self-imposed exile. Now they had the unenviable task of convincing her to virtually subjugate her identity to that of Sulana's. In effect, they were asking her to go into a new kind of "exile". Her decision would determine the success or failure of their attempt to heal Sulana Kay.

"Since you don't have a body, you must live as a spirit and that means that you cannot control the physical form that is Sulana," Zephron explained.

"What will happen to me? Tarsia asked, looking worried.

"That depends on you," Omega said. "If you resist letting Sulana's personality be the dominant one, you will in effect be imprisoning her soul in the same place where yours was trapped since you died as Tarsia."

Tarsia looked down at the ground with a pained expression. "Will I cease to exist?" she asked, tears welling in her eyes.

"No. Your individuated personality will eventually merge with that of Sulana's, but only when you re-incarnate. However, if Sulana agrees, it's possible that she will allow you to merge all your memories and previous life experiences with hers, but only if she accepts you as being part of her in this lifetime," Zephron said, and then added, "the decision to let you merge with her must be hers and hers alone. You cannot interfere."

"You're both one and the same, Tarsia. The only problem is that there are two of you with complete sets of individuated life experiences, but the physical body does belong to Sulana Kay and not you, after all," Waldo added.

"I'd like to offer you some comfort by telling you that time does not exist where you will stay until either Sulana accepts you or passes on," Carlatta informed her. "What I'm trying to say my love, is that you won't suffer as you have since your death as Tarsia. The place you were trapped in before was a place where you were stuck in a mental/psychological closed loop where your previous life memories kept repeating themselves over and over. If you voluntarily relinquish control of Sulana's life and body, your experience in the higher plains will be peaceful."

"Still, a part of you was able to re-incarnate as Sulana Kay and that indicates that somewhere in your higher bodies you were aware of the situation and did something about it," Zephron suggested.

"I feel as if I'm saying goodbye to you all, yet I don't feel the same sense of abandonment and fear that I experienced as the old me," Tarsia added.

"That's because your soul has healed itself and now, you're the truest representation of an individual's higher self, which after all, is what all beings truly are in the eyes of the Universal Mind God," Carlatta said, with emotion in her voice.

Tarsia's eyes suddenly lit up with understanding, and her expression transformed to one of peace and joy. She had come full circle and had reached sahmadi, (a state of complete peace) she was at one with the universe. Her body began to glow and became pure white light, the image of Tarsia's form dissolved, and Sulana's image reappeared where Tarsia's form had been.

As Tarsia began to disappear, Carlatta changed her form back to her current self.

Sulana opened her eyes and then raised her arms looking at her Gulax hands. Her expression was one of surprise. It was as if she was seeing her body for the first time. She turned around and then looked at the foursome sitting around her with a strange look on her face.

"What happened to the other girl?" she asked, referring to Tarsia.

"She left Sulana, she didn't want to be in the way," Zephron announced.

"Did I scare her away?" Sulana asked, looking sad. "I think I was mad at her, but I don't remember why." She paused for a moment and seemed to remember something important. "She wanted to tell me something, but I was scared for some reason and I wouldn't let her talk to me." She stopped talking, and then gasped while holding her hand to her mouth. "Oh, dear, I gagged her and tied her up and put her in a dark cave. How horrible of me! How could I have done such a thing?" she asked, looking around feeling guilty.

"Nothing bad happened Sulana. It was all a misunderstanding, and you don't need to be concerned about it at all," Waldo suggested, in a casual tone of voice.

Sulana looked at Carlatta and didn't recognize her. "I'm sorry, you must think terribly of me," she said apologetically. "My name is Sulana Kay, have we met before?"

"I don't think so Sulana. My name is Carlatta. I'm Waldo's mate. Pleased to make your acquaintance," she said, offering her hand.

"Likewise, I'm sure," Sulana replied, shaking Carlatta's hand and then suddenly becoming aware of the environment around her. "What is this place, how did I get here?" she asked, innocently.

Slowly, Zephron, Waldo, Omega and Carlatta explained to her what this place was and how she'd gotten there. At first, she naturally refused to believe what they were telling her was true, but after a while, as Zephron, and Omega made themselves disappear and re-appear again, she accepted what was going on.

They reassured her that everything was fine and that they would all be leaving this place together and that she would find herself in a medical facility back at the mansion. Omega also explained to her that her real body had been in a comatose state for almost three days and that when she "awakened" she would find herself bound hand and foot to an operating table and that she shouldn't panic and that the restrains would be taken off immediately. He added that she would be feeling very weak since she'd only been fed intravenously for the last three days. Sulana acknowledged that she understood.

"Are you ready Sulana?" asked Zephron.

Sulana seemed a little anxious, but she trusted the foursome. "Yes, I'm ready!"

The Gulaxian desert turned into the operating amphitheater at the mansion in the Ranes Valley on the Planet Centralia, and Sulana opened her eyes for the first time in three days.

CHAPTER 9

Rain and Salty Tears

You really don't have to wheel me around in this contraption," Sulana complained to Susan and Terence who were pushing her on an old-fashioned wheel chair out into the garden at the rear of the house.

"Sorry dear, doctor's orders. Om says that you're still weak from your experience and we're not about to contradict anything that Omega tells us to do!" Susan replied laughing.

"Om says one more day and then you can walk on your own again," Terence added gleefully as they passed through the green house's glass doors leading to the garden behind the mansion.

"I'm not used to be taken care of like this. I feel I'm such a burden already with me having caused such trouble with my coma and all."

"Yes, how dare you suffer a psycho-spiritual traumatic event in our house and ruin all our lives!" commented Susan with sarcastic humor as they reached the lawn.

"She really is inconsiderate, isn't she?" chimed in Terence trying to make a point.

"Alright you two, I'll shut up now it's obvious that you won't let me do anything by myself until tomorrow so I might as well relax and let you cater to my every whim for the next 24 hours."

"Good girl!" Susan said triumphantly, "Maybe now you'll allow yourself to have a good time."

"Here we are." Terence announced, when they reached the large picnic table that the mansion's house services had set up on the terrace by the waterfall. Several large café style umbrellas had been placed around the table providing shade for the twenty or so people who would be participating in the celebration of Sulana's recovery.

Behind the table by the pool fed by the waterfall, stood Carlos and Vardik laboring over a large portable barbeque station grilling several types of vegetables and animal flesh all of which produced a swirling cloud of smoke which rose and floated away toward the mountain range behind the mansion.

When Carlos and Vardik noticed the arrival of Sulana and company they put down their cooking utensils and came to the table.

"How are you Sulana!" both men said simultaneously, happy to see her.

"Fine thank you gentlemen," Sulana responded with a smile.

Vardik said a few more polite words and then he excused himself claiming that his zucchini needed to be turned over. Carlos remained behind holding Sulana's right hand. Sulana didn't feel the need to shy away from his large human hand which wrapped around her thin leathery hand like an elephant trunk.

"I owe you a debt of gratitude for your willingness to be a guinea pig to help cure me," Sulana said sincerely.

"Oh, it was nothing. All in a day's work for a super-hero like me!" Carlos said jokingly, but then turned serious. "Sulana, I would do anything for a family member. I'm so glad that you're back with us," he concluded, patting her small hand.

"Thank you Carlos. I know that you really mean what you say about me being family."

"It may take you a while to fully accept the truth that you are... were, Tarsia Rogeston my long-lost sister who once shared a house with me and the others on Plantanimus."

Sulana looked wistfully at the tall mountains shimmering in the distance from the warm midday air rising from the valley floor and mused philosophically on the issue. "There's a part of me that accepts the fact that I was once a flesh and blood member of the Rogeston family, but I'm afraid my lizard brain is struggling with the concept that I was once a half Terran half Tarsian humanoid."

"Give it time Sulana. It will all come together for you eventually," Carlos affirmed with conviction.

"I'm sure it will," Sulana replied, patting Carlos hand in return. She spoke confidently but her heart felt otherwise.

"Well I have to get back to my sausages and grilled corn on the cob otherwise they'll turn into charcoal!" Carlos announced, then returned to his barbequing duties.

Sulana looked toward the house and saw Waldo and Carlatta approaching the picnic area, each carrying a large tray full of various prepared food items. She closed her eyes and tried to imagine them as Kelem and Anima walking through the Dreamer Forest on Mount Olympus on Plantanimus, but her mind would not let her consider those two sets of individuals as a pair of people who were once her adoptive grandparents.

She felt uncertain about her future. Especially now that she had found that that she was once a Rogeston herself. Suddenly, her entire career as a galactic historian came into question. She was sure that she wouldn't publish her dissertation now. "What would be the purpose?" she asked herself cynically.

She was overwhelmed with feelings of guilt embarrassment and thoughts of failure. She was also beginning to feel trapped in this privileged paradise where everyone seemed to be so superior to everything and everyone that she ever knew before coming here. She had already decided that she would leave as soon as she was strong enough to walk on her own two feet. And she was dreading the moment when she would announce her decision to leave Centralia and return to Terra Prime.

For the time being she would continue pretending that everything was fine and tell everyone involved, exactly what they wanted to hear from her.

Yesterday she had to endure two difficult hours with Thula when she came to talk to her as she sat at the foot of her bed crying sadly for almost the entire time she stayed in her room. The poor girl went on and on about how the whole thing was all her fault and would Sulana please forgive her for pushing her too fast etc., etc. It was all too much!

Sulana did all she could to communicate to Thula that she didn't have any feelings of resentment toward her, which was true. However, her incessant requests to hear Sulana say that she forgave her again and again drove her to boredom. Sulana might have suffered a psychological traumatic event, but she was sure that Thula also needed psychiatric help.

She finally resorted to claiming that she didn't feel good and wanted to rest in order to get rid of Thula and be left alone in peace.

Terence had come by later that afternoon and apologized to Sulana for Thula's long stay in her room. He told Sulana that Thula had been told to be brief and not to stay more than a few minutes. Sulana claimed that it was no bother but she could tell that Terence was not happy with Thula's actions. Of all the members of the family she felt best when in the company of Terence, Susan and Carlos. A few days before she had felt very connected to Thula but something had changed now and she felt she needed to avoid the young Tarsian girl for her own good.

Waldo and Carlatta reached the picnic area and placed the large trays of food in the center of the big table. Waldo asked Sulana if she was hungry.

Sulana said yes, trying to sound upbeat.

"That's a good sign! It means you're getting better," Waldo affirmed feeling pleased.

"Thank you, Waldo. I do feel better," Sulana responded. Then, looking at the food tray she asked, "what's in the tray?"

"Oh, you know, the usual, potatoes, carrots, Tareean tubers, Tarsian Dewberries, stuff like that."

"Hmmm." Sulana exclaimed, feigning enthusiasm. "Everything looks wonderful, I can't wait to eat."

"You can pick before everyone starts eating if you want Sulana, don't be shy," Carlatta suggested.

Sulana reached for the tray in front of her and grabbed some vegetables in her hand and ate them with apparent gusto.

The rest of the picnickers arrived soon after and everyone sat down to eat. Sulana ate and talked to the others and listened politely to their conversation, pretending to be interested in what they were saying. Throughout the meal her mind kept wandering, and she had to force herself to focus on what each person was saying to her. At times she would say, 'yes; and 'is that so?', completely ignorant of what the person talking to her had just said. She felt distant and disconnected to everyone at the gathering as if she was watching the whole thing on a screen from a remote location. Physically, she felt as if she was sitting at the bottom of a swimming pool while everyone else was above the surface of the water trying to communicate with her.

The meal seemed to go on forever, and just when she felt that she couldn't fake one more polite answer to whatever inane question she had just been asked, people began drifting off and soon, Terence and her were the only ones left sitting at the table. Some of the guests were helping Vardik and Carlos clean up the portable barbeque, while Waldo and Carlatta had carried away the now empty trays of vegetables and fruits.

Terence regarded Sulana with the eyes of a therapist, aware that she seemed out of sorts. Throughout the meal he had glanced casually in her direction and noticed that she was doing a good job of behaving normally, but his training told him that it was all a façade.

"You look tired Sulana, would you like to go back to your room and get some rest?" he asked causally.

"Yes, thank you Terence. I do feel a bit drained. Perhaps a nap will do me some good," Sulana responded, grateful for his suggestion. All she wanted to do at the moment was to get away from everyone in the house.

Terence got up from his chair and came around to wheel Sulana back to the mansion. Halfway through the lawn just before they reached the entrance to the green house, Terence spoke again. "Perhaps you should stay in bed another day or so. It might do you some good."

"Oh no. I want to get back on my feet as soon as possible. You know I hate being carried around in this ridiculous wheelchair!" Sulana protested forcefully, but at the same time trying not to sound too upset.

"It's just that you looked a little overwhelmed by everyone talking to you back at the table. After all, you've just gone through a very powerful experience, and I don't think the others realize how strongly it has affected you."

"Wellm maybe a little," Sulana said, trying to make light of the situation. I guess I'm still adjusting to what happened to me three days ago. What I really want to do however, is to get back to my regular routine. I hate everyone making such a big fuss over me."

"You are part of the family and we naturally want to make sure that your recovery is one hundred percent," Terence added, as they entered the green house.

"I appreciate the care everyone is showering on me, but maybe there's too much going on here at the mansion. It might be better for me to go back to the house on Elmaru Road and recuperate there away from the all the activity and hubbub going on here."

"You may be right. But first, Omega wants to give you a final check up tomorrow to make sure that you'd be alright on your own. After that, I'm sure that he'd be alright with you going back to the house by the beach," Terence said confidently.

Sulana felt relieved to know that she might be able to leave the mansion by tomorrow. She dreaded having to tell everyone that she had decided to leave Centralia while still at the mansion. There would surely be pleads for her to stay for a longer period. Particularly, from Thula. Sulana didn't have the strength to deal with that pressure right now.

In a strange reversal of the past, it was she who was rejecting the Rogeston family this time, wishing to leave everyone behind.

There was a storm of conflicting emotions battling for supremacy in her conscious mind. A part of her felt betrayed by fate and circumstances for ruining what had once been a promising career as a galactic historian. Everything that she had fought and struggled for in her twenty six years of life seemed pointless now. Her book about the mystery of the ultimate fate of the Rogeston Clan seemed like a cruel joke played at her expense by the universe. Her feelings about her Gulax parents had been affected as well. Even though she was genuinely related to them by blood, she somehow felt as though she had suddenly been told that she had been adopted as a child. Her entire persona and confident self-image were now in question.

Yet in a strange way, she also felt liberated by the knowledge that she had once been Tarsia Rogeston. Her new found awareness of her previous life had brought back a torrent of memories. Perhaps some trace of that life had been responsible for bringing her here after all. In the last day or so, she had caught herself once or twice being surprised at seeing her Gulax face and body when she came past a mirror or a shiny surface. And there was a part of her (both as Sulana and Tarsia), that needed to know the entire history of the Rogestons from the time that she'd left Plantanimus as Tarsia Rogeston. The knowledge of that history would satisfy Sulana the historian and bring closure to Tarsia, the lost member of the family.

They had reached the door to the small elevator that led to the upper floors of the mansion. Terence entered first, walking backwards so that he could wheel Sulana forwards when the door opened on the top floor. They remained quiet during the ride, each absorbed in their own thoughts. The door opened to the hallway that led to her room which was but a few meters away. Once in the room, Sulana jumped up from the wheelchair and stretched her legs by walking around very energetically, almost as if to show Terence that she really didn't need the device at all.

Terence observed Sulana's sudden bout of physical activity and quickly realized that Sulana was not tired at all, but simply wanted to be left alone. "I'll leave you to rest now, do you want me to close the curtains?"

"Yes, thank you I could use some shut eye," she said, plopping herself on the bed and stretching her limbs."

"Sleep well Sulana. By the way, if you feel hungry when you wake up, call me on the intercom and I'll come up and take you down to the kitchen for some food, my extension is sixty-two."

"Thanks Terence, I'll do that," she answered as she slipped into the bed and pulled the covers up to her head.

Terence closed the curtains and the room darkened. He left shutting the door behind him. Sulana listened for the sound of his footsteps fading away as he walked to the elevator. As soon she heard the elevator door close, she jumped out of bed and went to one of the two large windows facing the garden at the rear of the mansion. She kneeled behind the curtain looking down at the garden as house-keeping service personnel where collapsing all the café umbrellas and taking them away. The time was two dash five, and for the first time since she'd arrived at the mansion the skies had turned grey. "Might as well be cloudy, it matches my mood," she thought to herself sullenly.

A gust of wind rattled the window pane and water droplets appeared on the glass surface. The sky grew darker and rain began to fall heavily. Down in the garden the workers were dashing through the grass carrying the last of the café umbrellas trying to escape the deluge.

Sulana felt something wet on her cheeks and thought for a moment that the heavy rain was coming through a crack in the window. She flipped her reptilian tongue to wipe the liquid from her face and was surprised to find that the taste of the water was salty.

Sulana was crying, and for a long time the tears would not stop.

CHAPTER 10

Last Check Up

Omega was examining Sulana's eyes with a retinoscope but she was fidgeting.

"Sulana please, keep your secondary eyelid open and stop moving about. I can't look into your retina if you don't keep still."

"Like our ears, Gulax eyes are also very sensitive to bright lights," Sulana responded annoyed.

"I know it will all be over in a couple of minutes," Omega said reassuringly.

After two more uncomfortable minutes, Omega turned the retinoscope off and switched the room lights on.

He led Sulana to another chair next to a wall of electronic equipment and attached a series of nano leads onto Sulana's chest, abdomen, head and wrists and turned on a virtual screen and keyboard floating three dimensionally on top of an analyzing machine. Sulana sulked feeling impatient. She didn't see the need for such a lengthy medical examination but at least now she didn't have to look at a blindingly bright light. Omega looked at the display on the screen showing heartbeat, blood pressure skin temperature etc. and typed in data regarding his patient.

After an hour of tests upon tests, she had grown bored and restless and wanted to be out of the examining room. She looked at Omega's receding hairline and aging skin and a question came to her mind.

"What is it like….?" she began saying, not sure how to finish the question.

"Huh, what do you mean?" he said absentmindedly, as he continued typing on the virtual keyboard floating below the screen.

Sulana searched for the right words. "I mean, what is it like to die and then be reborn remembering everything that you did in your previous life?"

Omega finished typing and disconnected all the leads from Sulana's body. He turned off the machine in front of him and turned to face Sulana. Sitting there wearing a physician's tunic he looked every bit a doctor, reminding her of her childhood pediatrician a human named Dr. Rekoff who was a specialist on Gulax physiology.

"Well, at first you don't remember much of anything because you're an infant and the brain is not capable of processing complex thoughts of any kind. However, after a year to a year and a half, the memories start flowing in, and by the time one of us is two to three years of age, most of the previous life experiences become fully inset."

"I had the concept that you. I mean, that all of the colony members were born talking, and speaking like an adult from the get-go," Sulana admitted.

Omega laughed softly and then smiled gently as he regarded Sulana the way an adult looks at a child. "To answer your original question, it's actually very hard. The reason is that you have the memories and experience of an adult inside the body of a toddler, and that toddler, no matter how smart and mature he or she may be mentally, has to deal with all the physiological processes of childhood, pre-pubescence, pubescence and eventually adulthood. I can't speak to what it would be like for a Gulax, since most of us have traditionally re-incarnated in humanoid bodies ever since we left Plantanimus."

"How many have chosen to return in the bodies of a different species?" Sulana asked, curious about how her own re-incarnation came to be.

"Well to begin with, every single Dreamer became a human during the exodus," Omega reminded her. "In any case, at that time, Tatiana's technology was only able to create humanoid forms, so we all became humans by necessity as well as by choice. But to be more specific, about a dozen of us are currently living in the bodies of other species such as Tareean, Bulonte and Trobolean. I should further clarify that each and every one of those individuals were former Dreamers. One of the original humans that came to Plantanimus and was reborn as a Plantanimal there, chose to return as a Tareean and had a negative life experience. It seems that humans and other humanoid species are very attached to the traditional mammalian form. After that individual's bad experience, none of the original humanoid members of the colony have chosen to come back as anything other than human."

"And I'm the only one that has come back as a Gulax," Sulana mused.

"So far, that is," Omega commented. "You obviously did not experience any discomfort living as a Gulax." Omega stopped himself short and suddenly looked concerned. "You're not having any difficulties in that regard now are you?"

"No, not at all. I'm still comfortable inside my own skin in spite of my recent experience."

"Good! I'm happy to hear that," Omega said, exhaling softly with relief.

"But it begs the question. Why was I able to be born as a different species while other humanoids have had problems with the switch?"

"I don't know. Perhaps that could be an area that you could specialize in, in the future," Omega suggested.

Sulana looked down at the floor looking dejected. "Right now, my future looks dim. I don't know what I'm going to do with my life."

"Give it time Sulana. It's understandable that you should feel confused after such a life altering experience. I'm sure that after a while you'll get back to your old self and finish your book on us Rogestons," Omega said with optimism.

"Really Omega?" Sulana asked sarcastically. "You think I should tell the galaxy at large about 'our family's dirty little secret'?" she said angrily, as she got up from the chair and began pacing around the room.

"What do you mean?" Omega asked confused.

"What do I mean?" she said in a high-pitched voice. "Should I tell any and all who'd care to hear my story about how 'we' Rogestons have cornered the market on immortality?" she asked looking at Omega with an angry expression.

"Is that what….?" Omega began asking but was interrupted by Sulana's continuing angry speech.

"Or that my dear sister Tatiana's technology gave everyone a one shot opportunity to live a little longer but not the chance to keep living on and on forever as we…. as you all have?" she concluded her fists clenched in anger."

She came back to her chair and sat down breathing heavily, tears welling in her eyes.

"Is that what you think is going on here?" Omega asked with surprise in his voice.

"I'm not sure what I think. But you can bet that everyone else out there will."

Omega rubbed his chin and watched Sulana as she tried to regain her composure. She was highly agitated and seemed very upset.

"I didn't mean to say that you should disclose the fact that we can do what we do. I meant to say that your book will be a highly acclaimed in-depth historical examination of an illustrious family and will probably be very helpful to your career as a historian."

Sulana let out a hiss/laugh meant to be sarcastic. "Don't you see Omega?" Sulana asked, this time walking up to the old man and looking straight into his eyes. "The definitive books on the Rogeston clan have already been written by no other than the illustrious Professor Zephron Artemus who just happens to be Zeus himself, your eldest Dreamer brother!" she said pointing her sharp lizard finger at his chest.

She sighed heavily and returned to her chair and sat down crossing her arms on her chest. After a few minutes, her breathing slowed down and she looked back at Omega apologetically.

"I'm sorry I yelled at you. I suppose that since you're not a graduate student/writer of galactic history you don't understand that the only thing that would have made my book anything other than a re-hash of

Zephron's books would have been my discovering what truly happened to the Rogeston Family after 2965!"

"I see." Omega said understanding Sulana's reason for her frustration. "It seems we've taken away your life's work and left you with nothing."

"That about describes it," Sulana retorted with sarcasm.

"Surely that's not so, Sulana! Aren't there other histories and mysteries that you can explore in the future? Other quests that will inspire you and bring you satisfaction and professional notoriety as a historian?"

"The muse is dead Omega!" she answered dryly, looking away.

Omega wanted to pull Sulana out of her dark mood but thought better of it. He didn't want to stress her any more that she was now. Perhaps Zephron or Waldo would be a more appropriate person to talk to her and help her out of her despair.

"What will you do?" he asked.

"I don't know what I'll do with the rest of my life. Right now, all I want to do is go back to my parent's house in Johannesburg and surround myself with all the familiar things that I've known in my life as Sulana Kay." She paused and looked at Omega with a strange look in her eyes. "Could you... could one of you erase my memory of ever having been here and remembering that I was once Tarsia?" she asked, her voice breaking.

Omega felt a deep pang of sadness brought on by Sulana's desperate request. He stood up from his chair and walked over to the single window in the room to avoid letting Sulana see his expression. When he managed to control his emotions he spoke softly, his face still turned away from her.

"To erase Tarsia's memories from your present consciousness would be like murdering her. You would continue living as Sulana Kay, but Tarsia's essence, in other words, everything that she ever was whether good, bad or indifferent would be lost forever. And later on when your present body dies, all that you are in this life as Sulana would also be lost forever."

He turned around and walked over to where Sulana was sitting her head down on her chest. He lifted her chin up as one does to a forlorn child and spoke gently and lovingly. "You see little one, you're both one and the same. No Dreamer has ever caused any living being any harm whatsoever, and therefore we could never grant your wish to forget Tarsia's life."

Sulana broke down in tears and wrapped her arms around Omega's waist her claws digging into Omega's side just short of breaking his skin as she shook sobbing, tightening her grip on the old man who had once been one of her closest friends back on Plantanimus.

She stopped crying after a while and realized that she was causing Omega pain with her sharp claws. She pulled her arms away from him and became upset to think that she had harmed him in any way.

"I'm sorry Om, did I hurt you? I don't know what came over me. I've never cried so much before. As a matter of fact, I never cried at all until I came here!" she said, feeling confused and angry at herself.

"Don't feel bad little one, I'm not hurt. Besides, no amount of physical pain could ever keep me from comforting you," he said, pulling his chair next to her and wrapping his arms around her narrow shoulders.

Sulana leaned her head on his shoulder and embraced him gently this time. They remained like that for a long while as Omega fought back his own tears. He knew they were about to lose Tarsia once again.

CHAPTER 11

One Last Conversation

Sulana stood by the windows facing the sea in the living room of the house on Elmaru Road. She had been back for three days now and was feeling more peaceful though in a melancholy, lonely sort of way. She had left the mansion on the same day of her final check up by Omega, and had quietly been brought back to the house late in the evening by Terence in the same buggy in which she had traveled to the mansion a week before. Vardik and Susan had been by every day since her return to Elmaru to bring her food, to checkup on her and bring her messages from Thula and the others. They had respected her decision to return to Earth and to be left alone in the house until her departure.

The following day after her return, she had tried to book passage to Earth on a Tareean freighter but Zephron would have none of it. He had already bought a ticket for her on a Tarsian luxury liner which would be departing sometime tomorrow morning and that was that. Personally, she was glad to avoid the cost of the trip and put up no objection to the special treatment. In a strange way, she felt she deserved to travel in utter luxury for once in her life.

Her meager belongings had been packed ever since she had returned to the house, and with nothing else to do, her days had consisted of sleeping long hours and watching entertainment vids on the giant screen in one of the living room walls.

This morning she had been told by Susan that Waldo would be coming over later tonight to talk to her before she left. It was two dash eight in the afternoon, and she expected that he would be arriving sometime during the third day period near sundown. She was sure that he was coming over to answer all the questions that were still foremost in her mind regarding the Rogeston family history following the exodus. Tarsia's memories were rather spotty from the time she left Plantanimus, and her recollections of the tragic life she led following her departure from the planet were difficult to contend with.

The day that Terence had driven her back to the house she had asked him if someone in the family could talk to her in detail about the past four hundred years before she left Centralia. Even though she was no longer interested in the Rogestons as a historian, she still had a great deal of curiosity as a former member of the family. There was much that she felt she needed to know for her own personal satisfaction.

Watching the ocean turn to a deep blue as the sun retreated westwards, she caressed the surface of the windowsill and recalled the moment that Thula had touched her hand in that same spot almost a week before. She had never felt a sensation like that. And even now, despite everything that had happened, some part of her retained a feeling of deep connection with her former sister. She wished that she could return Thula's need for affection, but Sulana could not deal with the emotions that her sister's presence brought out in her.

A strong wind was blowing from the east and the waves were unusually high today. The memory of an ocean that had once been familiar to her as a child on Plantanimus came to her in a rush, and for a moment she was transported to the old family beach cottage. She remembered playing with her older brothers and sisters frolicking in the water, screaming and yelling with great enthusiasm as children are prone to do in summer.

Standing by the edge of the water, she turned around and saw her mother and father sitting on the porch of the beach cottage, holding hands as they watched their children play on the beach. Sulana's throat tightened with emotion as she realized that this was nothing but a memory from her life as Tarsia. Her heart ached remembering how happy she had been living on the paradise that was Plantanimus so long ago. In contrast to those happy memories, her present reality seemed fractured and full of uncertainty.

The sound of landing thrusters brought her out of her nostalgic remembrance, and turning her head towards the rear of the house she saw Vardik's flyer land in the garden. The door opened up and Waldo stepped down carrying a small satchel on his shoulder. As soon as Waldo reached the main door to the house, Vardik lifted off heading in the direction of Landana the planet's capital.

Sulana rushed to the door to let Waldo in, and once inside the house, the two of them hugged each other warmly. Waldo's arrival had raised Sulana's mood as she was anxious to hear the true version of the story of the family's fate post exodus.

"Come in, come in! Would you like some tea?" she asked graciously, leading him by the arm.

"Yes, some tea would be nice especially on such a cold dreary day. Why don't we both go to the kitchen and make some?" he asked, rubbing his hands to take away the chill.

Once in the kitchen, Sulana made some tea and they both sat down in the tall chairs by the center island and slowly sipped from their cups remaining quiet for a while.

Waldo broke the silence first. "You have many questions and I'm here to answer any and all you may have," he said with a pleasant smile.

"I have so many, but the most obvious one is what happened after you left Plantanimus?"

"Well, first let me give you some background to the story. With the help of some of the most trusted members of the Conglomerate, we had been preparing for an exodus for many years before we actually left. Through the three hundred or so years that I lived on Plantanimus, I managed to amass a great deal of Galactic Kreds in preparation of such an event. Years before Alexei and Kani arrived, Zeus and I had seen the possible future that would become reality for Plantanimus. So, with the help of Queen Harriett and a few Conglomerate friends, I began to invest in the Terran and Tarsian markets and soon became a multi-trillionaire."

"Amazing!" Sulana uttered in wonder.

"When the time came to leave, we had three <u>*n-time*</u> cruisers of our own in orbit around Falmant the fifth planet in the Plantanimal Solar System, and that's how we left the planet. We began taking ten to twenty people up to the ships over a period of two weeks and soon after that, we were gone."

When did Alexei and Kani die?" asked Sulana, feeling regret for not ever seeing her parents again after she left Plantanimus as Tarsia.

"They died during the blockade in 2967. Alexei went first and Kani followed him three months later as is common with married couples who've lived together for so many years. Your parents were married for 102 years!"

Sulana looked out toward the ocean from the kitchen as tears flowed from her eyes.

"Don't feel bad Sulana," Waldo said, reaching for her arm affectionately. "They lived a wonderful life full of adventure and spiritual richness. And even though your absence affected them deeply, they never succumbed to despair or gave up on the hope that one day you'd rejoin the family. And look, here you are after all these years," he added with a smile.

"And now I'm leaving the family again just like I did before. It seems to be my modus operandi," Sulana said sarcastically, in an almost inaudible voice.

"This situation is different and bears no resemblance to what happened four centuries ago," Waldo said, leaning in and wiping a tear left on Sulana's right eye. "You were brought here by subterfuge and at the wrong time my sweet Sulana. Zephron, Omega and I found you through the quantum tide during one of our meditations, and we would have brought you in to the family in a more carefully planned and deliberate way, which would have produced a different result than what has occurred in the last few days."

"I don't understand," Sulana said confused. She had assumed that her being brought here had been sanctioned by Waldo, Zephron and Omega.

"Of all of us, your sister Tatiana was the most seriously affected by your disappearance. And through subsequent re-incarnations she has been obsessed with finding you and returning you to the fold. Unfortunately, Thula overheard us discussing our discovering that you were living on Terra Prime as a Gulax female. We decided to wait a decade before taking any action concerning you, and obviously that was too long for Thula. She took it upon herself without telling anyone and started the process of contacting you prematurely by sending a courier to Earth and planting that book of poems written by Zeus in that bookstore in Montevideo, knowing that once you found it, it would bring you to us sooner rather than later. Afterwards, she told us what she had done, and by that time we were left with no other choice but to let events unfold as they did."

"How would it have been different if you had done it the slow way?" Sulana asked curious.

"You would have never found Zeus' book of poems and your trip to Plantanimus would have been the end of your investigation on the family. Then we, and by that, I mean one of us, probably Omega or myself, would have traveled to Terra Prime, located you and made contact. Then slowly over a period of years, we would have prepared you to deal with the knowledge of your previous incarnation."

"I understand. But now I have another big question. It's something that's been bothering me greatly and I hope that you'll answer me honestly," Sulana said with emphasis. "Why hasn't the family shared the technology that allows you to purposely re-birth individuals with full awareness of their previous lives with the rest of the galaxy?"

"I will be totally honest with you. But first be aware that the answer is complicated, so bear with me," Waldo said, standing up from his chair and then putting his empty teacup in the kitchen sink. He returned to his seat and looked up at the ceiling as if trying to remember something.

"To begin with, four hundred years ago, Plantanimus was almost destroyed by the warring factions vying for possession of the planet, and as you know, they nearly succeeded. We realized then that whoever took over the planet once the conflict was settled, would become the most powerful force in the known galaxy and would use the power of bestowing immortality to others as a way of controlling and manipulating all the other nation planets. They would give themselves total access to the ability of re-incarnating as Plantanimals and would charge others huge amounts of money for the opportunity to live forever. In other words, the Dreamers would have become nothing but slaves to the conquerors of Plantanimus and would have spent the remainder of their natural lives as factories of Plantanimal bodies for their masters."

"I never thought much about the consequences of Plantanimus falling under the rule of a conqueror and the subsequent enslavement of the planet. Still, that doesn't answer my question, since the Dreamers are no longer in their original bodies and are now living as free willing ambulant humanoids," Sulana argued logically.

"I'm afraid you don't understand Sulana," Waldo interjected. "The so called 'technology' that you refer to, is dependent on all the former Dreamers remaining in close physical proximity to one another every time one of us is reborn. Furthermore, their mental and psychic powers were greatly reduced the moment they were transferred to human bodies. Now more than ever, they must remain close to one another in order to accomplish that goal."

"So, it takes all one thousand of them together in one place to re-birth someone?" Sulana asked.

Waldo looked sad for a moment before he answered her question. "There are no longer one thousand individual souls once known as Dreamers, Sulana," he said shaking his head. "Unfortunately, during the blockade, Plantanimus was bombarded with energy weapons on and off for many years and several Dreamer 'brethren' died as a result of their injuries."

Sulana suddenly felt as if she had just been told that a close friend of hers had died unexpectedly. During her time on Plantanimus as young Tarsia she had given names to several dozen Dreamers near Kelem and Anima's cottage. Omega, the youngest, had always been her favorite but she had grown fond of many of the other older Dreamers as well. "I didn't know," Sulana said surprised at how deeply the news of the passing of some of the Dreamers was affecting her.

"So, as you can see, not only do all the former Dreamers need to be together to do their work, most of them cannot live apart from the remaining survivors of the original group for too long. Except for Zephron, Omega and ten others, the rest have not been able to individuate themselves sufficiently to become separate beings on their own."

How many of them survived?" Sulana wanted to know.

"Seven hundred and eighty-four are still with us, including Zephron and Omega. We lost two hundred and sixteen during the blockade."

Sulana was shocked to hear how many had perished. "That many?" she whispered, her voice trailing off.

"During that time I felt the effects of the death of the ones that died whenever I communed with Zeus. It was the most viscerally painful and deep sense of loss that I ever experienced, despite all the tragedy that I endured in my life as Kelem Rogeston."

"It must be very painful to lose someone that you've known and loved for over ten thousand years," Sulana said quietly, her mind trying to imagine what it must have been like for the surviving Dreamers.

"Now do you begin to understand why we keep to ourselves?" Waldo asked.

"I'm sorry that I pre-judged you without asking what the reasons for all the secrecy was. Now I understand why Zephron and the rest of you have kept your true identities hidden from the world at large and remained so close to one another all these centuries."

"There's more that you need to know Sulana. There are other forces outside of the immediate family's concerns, and the practical interests of the colony that are motivating us and inspiring us to work for the benefit of all other living beings in the galaxy."

"I'm glad to hear that the Rogestons have altruistic motives other than self-preservation on their agenda," Sulana said with relief.

"Indeed. And what I'm about to tell you is perhaps more sensitive in nature than all of the secrets of the Rogeston family and the Dreamers put together."

Sulana's ears pulled back. She was surprised to hear that there would be an even more important secret in the universe other than the true nature of the Universal Mind God or the secret of immortality!

"About five hundred years ago, just before the blockade of Plantanimus, Zeus and the others began to sense a looming threat that seemed to originate from very far away. For a long time, I assumed that what they were 'feeling' or 'seeing' as a future conflict, was related to the coming blockade of Plantanimus which Zeus and the others had already foretold. But as the blockade unfolded and the years went by, they continued talking about this "threat" as being a separate event from the troubles that we were enduring at the time. Strangely enough, the death and destruction of their fellow Dreamers during this period when the bombardments began, gave the surviving members of the colony a kind of psychic boost. During a month-long period, Zeus and the rest began to get clear messages concerning the "threat" that they had been telling me about."

"What was it that they were seeing?" Sulana asked, completely enthralled by the mystery.

"What they saw was a threat to all the inhabitants of the Milky Way Galaxy," Waldo said somberly.

"You mean like an invasion of some sort?" She suggested.

"Yes. An invasion from an unknown species. And they're coming Sulana, of that we are sure." Waldo said with conviction.

"Well, what do they want from us that they couldn't possibly find in their own galaxy?"

"They're pariahs. An evil group that was been exiled from their galaxy by their own people. They've been traveling towards the Milky Way for many eons and they're due to arrive ten thousand years from now."

"If we know they're coming, don't we have enough time to prepare a large military force to oppose them when they get here?" Sulana asked, not understanding why Waldo and the others thought that these aliens represented such danger.

"Weapons won't deter these aliens, Sulana. They're a cast of practitioners of evil and black magic, much like the Tau priests that once ruled, and eventually destroyed most of the life on Plantanimus. Besides, even if we were to warn everyone about them, most species would either not believe us or just plain ignore our warning."

Sulana's blood ran cold. Through her research on Plantanimus, she knew better than most people of the terrible holocaust that the Tau priests brought about with their overwhelming psychic powers. Their acts of depravity and cruelty were considered the most heinous and horrible deeds ever committed by anyone in the history of the Milky Way. She also knew that ten thousand years was but an instant when it came to the history of the universe. In terms of galactic history, the aliens were practically knocking at the front gates of the Milky Way.

"How are we going to stop these horrible beings from enslaving us all?" Sulana asked, hoping to hear an encouraging answer from Waldo.

"That's where the Dreamers, the Rogeston family and the rest of the colony come in," Waldo affirmed with passion. "We are the only ones that can prepare the population of our galaxy to fight these invaders by making everyone as psychically gifted and spiritually strong as the Dreamers once were. If we succeed in our quest, then the invaders will wash against our shores as a weak tide instead of an overpowering tsunami. Black magic and evil cannot thrive in the absence of fear and intimidation."

Sulana sat quietly reflecting on what Waldo had just told her and looked troubled. "There's something about your answer that troubles me Waldo. You said that we are the only ones that can prepare the population of the Milky Way to fight these invaders by making everyone as psychically gifted and spiritually strong as the Dreamers once were. Did you mean to imply that the Dreamers are not as powerful as they need to be in order to help everyone prepare to fight these devils?"

Waldo smiled wryly and nodded his head knowing that he had to explain the situation to Sulana in more detail.

"Yes and no. I told you that the answer to some of your questions would be complicated. Let me clarify. Our mission, the thing that we have been striving for these past four hundred years, is to recreate a new generation of Dreamer colonies in a series of terraformed planets throughout the Milky Way Galaxy. Once established and fully sentient, those Dreamers would form a powerful line of defense against the invaders. Their psychic power would enhance the abilities of the galaxy's population, whose spiritual vibrations would have been raised."

"Do you mean to say that you intend to grow a new batch of sentient plants that you're going to place all over the galaxy?" Sulana interrupted, thinking that she hadn't understood what Waldo had said.

"Precisely." Waldo answered.

"How can that be? I've stood next to the dead carcasses of the Dreamers in the forest on Mount Olympus. And wasn't the creation of the Dreamers an accidental fluke brought about by a dangerous combination of black magic, geological forces and a very powerful nature elemental conjured up from the bowels of Plantanimus?" Sulana asked, with incredulity showing in her face.

"Yes but…"

"It sounds like you're going to recreate the same kind of horror that you say you intend to save us from!"

"Relax Sulana!" Waldo countered, holding back a smile after her passionate outburst. "No evil incantations or powerful elementals are going to be conjured up by me or anyone else in the colony! Do you remember the night-blooming orchids that bloomed at the green house a few nights ago?" Waldo asked with a calm voice.

"Yes, of course I do! It was the memory of a similar species of flowers on Plantanimus' Dreamer forest that triggered my psychic coma as I suddenly remembered my previous life."

"Well, those flowers were engineered reproductions of the original species from Omega's research." Waldo stated raising his eyebrows expectantly at Sulana.

It took a moment for Sulana to put two and two together, and then her eyebrows went up. "Oh, I see! You're saying that Omega has found a way to grow new Dreamer bodies?"

"We're not quite there yet. But your arrival at the mansion the other night happened to coincide with Omega's breakthrough in his research. Although the flowers are far simpler organisms than a Dreamer body, the science is not. Omega has spent the last two hundred years looking for a way to recreate the DNA of the old Dreamer form."

"How close is he to growing a new generation of Dreamers?" Sulana asked.

"Very close. Within a few years, he'll have all the elements worked out."

"And then?" Sulana asked expectantly.

"And then, it will only be a matter of transporting all the seedlings to their corresponding terraformed planets, planting them at the proper elevation, adding sun and water and let nature take its course!" Waldo concluded smiling.

"But will that guarantee that those artificially grown Dreamers will achieve sentience on their own?" Sulana wondered.

"No of course not. Each planet will have a resident member of the colony trained specifically to interact with the young dreamers to help them achieve consciousness and also act as a teacher."

"How many planets are we talking about?" Sulana asked, feeling dubious about the entire scheme.

"Approximately eighteen hundred," Waldo said with a straight face.

Sulana couldn't help but laugh at the unrealistic scheme that her former grandfather had just described to her. It took over a hundred years with current technology to terraform a planet, not to mention the cost of the entire operation, plus the insurmountable mountain of legal paperwork and the acquisition of thousands of permits necessary to claim possession of a planet through the Galactic Counsel.

Being the daughter of a set of parents who were professional Terraformers, she knew a lot about the subject. She figured that the Rogestons might be lucky to complete fifty or sixty planets in ten thousand years, not to mention the fact that no one group or organization in the entire Milky Way was wealthy or powerful enough to afford the astronomical costs of such a gargantuan project.

For the first time in nearly a week, Sulana felt like her old self again. She composed herself and felt a little embarrassed by her hysterical fit of laughter.

"Forgive me Waldo. I didn't mean any disrespect. But I couldn't help but laugh at the incongruity of your plan," Sulana added apologetically. She hoped that Waldo hadn't taken offense from her reaction.

"I'm glad to see you laugh Sulana," Waldo said earnestly. "I've been a little worried about your mental state. Your laughter proves to me that you're going to be fine. I'm glad to see that you still have a sense of humor."

Turning serious, Sulana continued. "Honestly Waldo, even with all of yours and Zephron's money, you couldn't seed more than a dozen planets, and then there's the time factor to consider," she pointed out.

Waldo leaned back in his chair, clasped his hands and leaned his chin on them.

A mischievous smile appeared on his lips. He suddenly looked like the cat that ate the canary.

"What?" Sulana said, looking at him, sensing that a surprise might be forthcoming.

"Have you heard of the following organizations before? Waldo asked rhetorically. "Futuric Systems, The National bank of The Solar Nations, The Bank of Centralia, The Galactic Property Management Group, The National Bank of Mars, Apex Terraforming Consortium, General Thermodynamics and Space Vessel Manufacturing, The Altenian Cruise Lines, Nano Technologies Research Labs, Terra Prime Investment Bank, The National Bank of the United Tareean States, The Bank of Africa, The Lunar Water and Electric Company, Martian Water Works, Con Ed Terra, Con Ed Luna, Con Ed Mars and all the other electrical power grid suppliers on every know planet also named Con Ed?" Waldo concluded, after naming all the organizations almost with a single breath.

"I recognize most of them, and, Apex Terraforming, the largest terraforming corporation in the entire galaxy. They are responsible for creating more M-Class planets than any other outfit. As a matter of fact, my parents have worked for Apex most of their lives. Why did you ask me if I recognized those names? All of those are obviously the most powerful banking, manufacturing and utility companies in the known galaxy," Sulana said somewhat puzzled.

"Those are but a few of the businesses that the colony currently owns and manages," Waldo said demurely. "The total list consists of over five hundred large corporations, about twelve hundred medium sized corporations, and over six thousand smaller businesses. We also own several billion acres of real estate on about ninety six colonized planets, and we have legal claim to three thousand Earth sized uninhabited planets and planetoids spread out all over the Milky Way.

It takes a lot to truly shock a Gulax. Not only did Sulana's ears pull back severely, but her eyes became round spheres of black with gold flecks.

Sulana was speechless at the immense value of each and every one of the corporations and businesses that Waldo had just informed her were owned by the colony. She tried to figure out the total worth of the entire list of holdings, but the numbers were too high to figure out without a wrist comp even for a sharp minded lizard like Sulana.

"You own all those organizations and property?" she asked, her mind still struggling with the concept of such immense wealth and power. No one in history had ever possessed such ridiculous amounts of money, and if they had, they would have used it to rule the rest of the inhabitants of the Milky Way. Sulana realized at that moment how incredibly unusual it was for a group of individuals such as the colony members, to know that they were the richest people in the galaxy and yet, have remained cloistered together for over six hundred years and not have used that wealth to abuse and control others.

"How were you able to acquire such wealth and yet remain anonymous for so long?" Sulana asked logically.

"I established hundreds of holding companies under various identities during the 28th century and let them lie dormant for several decades. When the time came, I began to hire top notch management talent through third party sources and gave the top executives of each company a handsome salary and the financial resources necessary to succeed. I only invested in businesses that had high potential for growth and sold or closed those that didn't succeed within the first three years of their corporate life. Those original holding companies were the foundation upon which the wealth of the colony was acquired over the centuries. Over the years, different members of the colony assumed control of different boards of directors, and since they are all truly "new persons" each time they take over control of the business, no one has ever had a reason to suspect that the true ownership of all those assets is connected to us."

Sulana shook her head in amazement. "And all this time my parents were employees of one of your companies!"

"Actually you should be saying "our companies" Sulana. Despite your absence during the past five centuries, we've kept an escrow account open for you and we've been depositing a one hundredth of a percent portion of all our profits into that account every year since your departure from Plantanimus. All in the hope that one day you'd return to us."

"Are trying to tell me that I'm rich?" Sulana asked bewildered.

"All you have to do is lay claim at the Bank of Centralia and the money is yours," Waldo answered with a wide smile.

Sulana thought that she was about to fall prey to another psychic coma. She felt dizzy and even though she was sitting, she held on to the counter in the center island of the kitchen for dear life. After a few moments she calmed herself and spoke nervously. "Oh no! I couldn't take that money Waldo I didn't work for it. That money belongs to the family and all the other members of the colony who have worked very hard for it I'm sure!"

Waldo nodded understanding her reaction. "I understand how you might feel about this. We can't force you to take the money but just remember that it's there for you whenever you decide to use it."

"Please Waldo, close the account and split the money among the colony!" Sulana begged.

"I can't and I won't. Anyway, no one would accept the money. Face it Sulana, the money is yours. Perhaps in time you'll change your mind."

"You know the saying; "be careful what you ask for, you just might find it?" Sulana mused looking troubled.

"Yes of course."

Well, right now I wish that you hadn't answered any of my questions and simply had sent me on my way," she said wryly.

Waldo smiled and looked at Sulana with amusement. "Let's forget about the money, and as far as I'm concerned, you'll never hear another word about it from me. Is that OK?"

"Thank you!" Sulana said relieved. "It's not that I'm ungrateful. But I could never take a single Kred out of that account. I could never live with myself after that!" she added emphatically.

"Understood." Waldo noted. "I'm sorry that we got off on a tangent just now. I'm sure that there are other questions that you'd like answers to?"

Sulana thought about it for a second or two and realized that she still wanted to hear the full account of the family's plans.

"Back to the Dreamer project, in spite of all the wealth and power available to you, it still seems like a daunting prospect to me, Waldo," Sulana commented. How can you possibly accomplish such an enormous task?"

Waldo thought for a moment and then spoke. "Faith, time and destiny Sulana that's how."

Sulana tilted her head questioningly.

"First, we have an unending faith in God the ruler of the universe. Every man woman and child in the colony feels this way. Second, we have ten thousand years to reach our goal and we're very experienced in the business of working in terms of very long-time scales. And third, there are no coincidences in the universe Sulana. Even before I was born, my path and the path of the Dreamers, Alexei's, Kani's, yours, your brothers and sisters' and the rest of the members of the colony, were already laid out for us. Why the Universal Mind God chose all of us to do this work, is not for us to ask. But the one thing that we're all certain of, is that we were chosen to do this work and we live with the certainty that it will be done."

Until a week ago Sulana had held an agnostic point of view on God and religion. Being lizards, her parents viewed the world in the same way. But after her recent experiences, her concept of faith, spirituality and God was in flux. Waldo's belief in the certainty of his destiny struck a chord in Sulana's heart. Her world had always been a tidy logical place. Now everything had changed. Her concept of reality had expanded beyond anything that she ever imagined. Now the universe looked strange and her future seemed uncertain.

Sulana suddenly felt exhausted both physically and mentally. She had reached a point of information overload and her curiosity had been more than satisfied.

Waldo noticed her mood change and knew instinctively that enough had been said.

He looked at his wrist-comp and saw that it was three dash four. Outside, the winter sun had disappeared, and night had fallen. The wind had picked up and the waves on the beach had become frothy and wild.

"Are you all packed Sulana?" Waldo asked, bringing her out of her pensive mood.

Sulana snapped back to reality. "What? Oh yes, I don't have much, so I've been packed ever since I came back to the house," she answered absentmindedly.

Waldo reached for the satchel that he had brought with him and put it on his lap.

"I have a parting gift for you," he said, and then smiling he added, "and no, it's not money but something far more precious."

Sulana's eyebrows rose wondering what the gift could possibly be.

Waldo reached into the leather satchel and produced a finely carved wooden box thirty by twenty centimeters. The gilded artwork was done in typical Tarsian style full of plant and animal motifs. It looked very old.

"What is it?" Sulana asked, appreciating the antique's beauty.

Waldo opened the lid and the glow of two crystal orbs reflected on Sulana's reptilian eyes.

"They're memory orbs, the blue one belongs to Carlatta and me and it contains all the memories of our lives from the time that Anima came into my life up until now."

"And the other one?" Sulana asked her voice breaking with emotion.

"The other one is Tarsia's. It has all of her memories from the time she was born to the time she left Plantanimus."

"You're giving me these orbs to take with me?" Sulana said breaking into tears.

"Yes Sulana. No amount of conversation can replace a memory orb. You need to experience all that we've known since you left and later when you're ready, you will need to remember Tarsia's life. Only then will you be able to make sense of everything that has happened to you in this life, as well as your previous one. You need to heal the scar in your soul."

Sulana took the box from Waldo and he reached over and kissed her on her forehead and hugged her gently.

"I'm leaving now. I have to get back to the mansion. I hope with all my heart and soul that someday at some point in the future, you'll return to Centralia to visit us, or perhaps to stay with us for a season or two. Remember that you're family and are always welcome here no matter how much time has passed. Send us a message once in a while so that we know how you're doing and remember that you are dearly loved by all of us."

Waldo took his satchel and Sulana stood up from her chair and the two walked arm-in-arm toward the front door. Upon reaching the foyer, Sulana embraced Waldo tightly and held on to him for a long time.

She pulled back from him and looked into his eyes, then spoke in a soft voice. "Thank you, grandfather. You've always been there for me and I only wish that I could stay here with you and grandmother and the family, but my mind is confused, and I need to find myself once again."

"Don't cry child," Waldo said holding up Sulana's chin. "We love you no matter what your form or circumstances are. We are always with you even when you're thousands of light years away. Just think of us and know that we're thinking of you."

Waldo turned around, opened the door and walked out quickly into the cold wind lest Sulana see him crying. He got into the electric buggy parked behind the house, turned on the driving lights and drove off in the direction of Ranes Valley.

Sulana went back into the house. She closed the foyer door and then sat on the living room couch holding on to the wooden box for a long time.

The following morning just before dawn, Carlo's big shuttle landed on the garden's landing pad shaking the house with the sound of its huge thrusters. Sulana was ready with her light baggage and Carlos escorted her to the ship after she locked up the house. Before she climbed into the cabin, she turned around and took one last look at the beautiful house where she'd been staying. Its exterior lights were glittering in the cold morning air and she wished that she could have lived there.

The flyer lifted off and soon the ship reached the edge of the planet's atmosphere. She looked out of the cabin window at Centralia rotating slowly below, as Carlos guided his ship toward the loading dock of the Trian, a Tarsian luxury cruiser parked in stationary orbit above Centralia. She'd be traveling back to Terra Prime in the lap of luxury, but none of that seemed important now. Sulana looked down at the planet and felt as though a part of her had been left behind.

CHAPTER 12

A Sister's Goodbye

The following morning, Waldo gave Thula a hand written letter from Sulana. She opened the letter with a half-smile on her lips. Hardly anyone wrote by hand anymore and when she opened the first page, she was pleased to see Sulana's neat and artistic penmanship.

Dear Thula:

I wish that things would have turned out differently for all of us. I know than nothing would please you more than having me stay in Centralia permanently but that cannot be.

Even after remembering my former life and the history that connects me to the Rogeston family I can't abandon the family that I've known and loved in this life.

Until a week ago, I thought I knew what my life's direction was. But after my recent experience, my future seems to be in free fall. I need time to myself to figure out what it all means.

Please don't allow yourself to feel guilty about what's happened to me. As I've said before, I don't bear you any ill will. Perhaps our destiny is already decided by the universe.

I've never told you, but I feel very connected to you in a very special way. I don't know whether to call it a spiritual connection or something else, but it's as close as I've ever come in my life to think of such things. I've never been religious or spiritual. However, in the last few days I've experienced things that I never thought possible.

Thula, I don't know where destiny will take us, or whether we'll ever see each other again. Whatever happens, I'm sure to remember the time we spent together, and I know I'm going to miss your company as well as that of the rest of the family.

Live a good life and continue the important work that you're all doing. Waldo explained to me the details of your long tern goals and our personal problems seem so utterly unimportant by comparison.

Your sister, Sulana

Thula folded the letter and placed it gently on her lap, she looked up at the morning sky and whispered softly; "Goodbye my sister. I will always love you".

CHAPTER 13

"July 15ᵗʰ 3285"

The year was 3285 and the family was celebrating the summer solstice. The terraforming of Centralia was almost finished and it would be but a mere decade until the last of the three oceans on the planet would be completely formed. The weather had become warmer ever since the second ocean had been completed a few years before, and summer was now a warm and pleasant season planet wide. The temperature in Ranes Valley was positively tropical during this time of year.

Because of the multiple races and the individual cultures inhabiting the planet, the twelve months of the year were referred to as plain numerals, however the colony always used the ancient Gregorian Earth calendar, and today was the fifteenth of July, 3285.

The large garden behind the mansion had been converted to an impromptu amusement park complete with carnival rides and booths offering all sorts of foods, games and amusements.

There had been a rash of births among the colonists in the last twenty years, and for the first time in four centuries children almost outnumbered the adults. Waldo had designed and built a park next to the garden with a large swimming pool, swings, jungle gyms, slides and game courts to accommodate the growing number of youngsters.

Thula was seventeen years old when Sulana left Centralia in 3259. Now, twenty-six years later she was the mother of a boy named Alexei sixteen years old and a girl named Sulana thirteen years old. She met a Terran named Elijah in 3269 and had fallen madly in love with him and the two were married within a year of meeting each other. For the first time in centuries Thula had become a mother again and was enjoying life.

Waldo and Carlatta had also become parents during this time and they now had two boys, one named Zeus, thirteen years old and a younger one named Ndugu, nine years old.

Zephron, now forty-five years, old and Omega still sprite and youthful looking at ninety four, had remained bachelors, too busy with their work to take time for marriage and children.

Thula had languished for years after Sulana's departure, struggling to regain her old style and confidence in spite of all the efforts made on her behalf by Waldo and the others to bring her out of her melancholic state. But when Elijah arrived on Centralia to work as a research assistant for Zephron Artemus, everything changed for her. The Terran's kind and gentle personality had a positive effect on Thula, and within a few months she began to laugh and enjoy herself again. And because they both worked together as Professor Artemus' assistants, a romance soon flowered which led to marriage. A deeply spiritual person, Elijah was welcomed to the colony with open arms. Zephron, Waldo and the rest of the family knew they could trust him implicitly and he was eventually told the true identity of the family and the colony's plans for the future.

For the past few weeks Thula had been kept very busy organizing all the events and the hiring of professional entertainers and food vendors for the celebration. Waldo had asked her if she would volunteer for the job and she obliged.

It had all been Waldo's idea that from now on the colony should celebrate the summer season with a big party, "mainly for the children" he had said, but she suspected that he meant it for the adults as well.

Sitting at the gazebo by the waterfall, Thula, Elijah, Waldo and Carlatta were engaged in conversation amidst the noise of the crowd and the children's screams of delight as magicians, clowns and other performers entertained the crowd.

"Oh, Waldo this was such a great idea! And Thula's done such a great job getting it all organized," Carlatta exclaimed with a smile.

"Thank you Carlatta. I've really enjoyed putting it all together but I have to say that Alexei and Sulana worked almost as hard as I did. They really got into it and did a lot of research themselves when it came to finding the right entertainment for the kids!" Thula replied.

"Leave it to children to know better than adults what children really want," Waldo added.

"I was amazed by their tenacity and focus when it came to organizing this. I knew my children were smart and well behaved, but this really tops it all!" Elijah said proudly.

"Zeus and Ndugu put in a lot of hours in this project as well," commented Thula with a pleased look. "We might have the beginnings of a new group of corporate managers here!" she concluded.

"Not so far from the truth, Thula. A few days ago, I heard Alexei and Zeus discussing plans to attend one of the big colleges on a Davian King planet," Waldo announced.

"Really? They must have been talking about some sort of business management school. I know that Alexei wants to work in agricultural management. He worships Omega and his work," Elijah commented.

"What a difference from the first Rogeston generation of kids on Plantanimus. These kids can't wait to leave the nest!" Waldo said with a laugh.

The foursome laughed together, pleased with the way the day was turning out. Waldo looked at his wrist comp and quickly glanced at the crowd.

"I noticed you looking at your comp several times this morning Waldo. Are you expecting someone?" Thula asked.

"I invited some folks from town to join us and I'm just wondering where they are," Waldo responded.

Thula found it strange that Waldo should be so concerned about guests arriving at the party. He usually didn't pay attention to such mundane details but then again, he seemed very keen on this "solstice celebration" being a total success. The planning of the party seemed to have had a strong effect on everyone in the family. A sense of joy and happiness had taken over the entire colony in the last few weeks. Even Vardik, her normally introverted brother had shown signs of excitement.

Waldo and Carlatta left the gazebo at one point only to return with Susan, Terence and Carlos. They had brought some food and drink from one of the booths, and all seven ate the delicious fare and continued talking and enjoying themselves. Thula wished that Zephron and Omega could have joined them, but both were at a critical point in one of their projects and had cloistered themselves in Zephron's lair up on the mountain behind the mansion.

She looked up at the ridge where Zephron's compound was, its large green house dome shining brightly in the late morning sun. High above the mountain's crest, a metallic glint in the blue sky caught her attention as it seemed to be approaching the valley from the west. After a minute or so, the ship's outline became visible and Thula could hear the roar of its landing thrusters becoming louder as it descended toward the mansion's landing field just behind the waterfall. She turned around to look at the others wondering who it could possibly be that was approaching the house. She didn't recognize the particular ship that was now hovering high above the mansion positioning itself for a landing. It was then, that she noticed that they were all smiling at her and looking at each other with anticipation. The adults and the children in the garden had all stopped their revelry and were now walking slowly toward the landing field en mass.

Confused, Thula asked. "What is going on?"

Everyone in the gazebo stood up and Waldo extended his hand toward Thula. "Don't you want to know who it is that's about to land?" he asked with a sneaky smile.

Thula took Waldo's hand and followed him up the stairs onto the landing field as the crowd of about two hundred members of the colony assembled at the bottom of the waterfall. Behind her stood Carlatta, Elijah, Susan and Terence with a look of anticipation in their faces.

The beautiful gleaming ship began to come down slowly, its powerful turbines raising dust as it gently touched the ground. After a moment, the engine's high-pitched whine faded away and as the dust settled, a door opened on its right side. Part of the door turned into a small set of steps and the pilot stepped down to the field. The pilot began to walk toward the top of the waterfall where Thula and the others were gathered, and as the figure came near, Thula's eyes widened with shock and surprise when she realized that it was Sulana!

Her heart began to beat fast and her legs weakened at the knees as Waldo steadied her.

Sulana jumped up the steps onto the little bridge that crossed the stream that fed the waterfall and ran into Thula's arms. The crowd burst into a wild cheer and at the same time, music began to play and a volley of fireworks exploded high above the garden.

Thula was dumbstruck and could only cry silently as she embraced Sulana with all her might. The crowd broke into applause and the two women were led down into the garden by Waldo and Carlatta.

"You're here, you're really here!" Thula finally managed to whisper in Sulana's ear.

"Yes Thula, I'm really here." Sulana answered emotionally.

It was only then that Thula realized that this "celebration" was a welcoming party for Sulana's arrival. She marveled at the fact that the entire colony had been able to keep her in the dark for so many weeks.

"Welcome back Sulana," Waldo said hugging her warmly. "You haven't changed at all! You look exactly the same as the day you left!"

"Well you know lizards age very slowly!" she responded with a smile. "Whereas you, Thula... you've grown into a lovely woman," she said turning to Thula with appreciation in her eyes.

"I'm older and fatter but wiser!" Thula said laughing and crying with joy.

"I heard you married and have two children of your own," Sulana said.

"Yes, this is Elijah my wonderful husband," she said, reaching for Elijah's hand and pulling him from behind the others so that Sulana could meet him.

"A pleasure to meet you Sulana. We've all been looking forward to this day, and I know that you've made my wife very happy by coming here today," Elijah added.

Sulana thanked him and hugged him, then one by one the rest of the family welcomed Sulana while she and Thula held on to each other's arms. A very long picnic table was put up and nearly all the assembled party goers sat down for a celebratory meal to welcome the honored guest. All the while as several colony members came by and introduced themselves to Sulana speaking words of welcome, the two women held each other's hand as if afraid to let go. When things quieted down as the party began to wind down in the late afternoon, Sulana and Thula walked over to the gazebo and sat down next to each other.

Years before, they had both sat on this very same place under different circumstances.

"I didn't think that I would see you again," Thula confessed.

"For a long time, I didn't think that I would ever return, but here I am!" Sulana said spreading her arms.

"What changed your mind?" Thula asked.

"The day I left Centralia, Waldo gave me three memory orbs to take with me, his and Carlatta's and Tarsia's," she said turning her gaze to the waterfall. "For years I didn't touch them because I was afraid."

"What were you afraid of?" Thula asked.

Sulana looked back at Thula with a wistful look. "I was afraid to remember my old life, but I was even more afraid to know what Kelem and Animah and the rest of the family had felt and experienced as a result of my absence. Tarsia's personality and memories began to blend with my consciousness soon after I left Centralia. Her long held feelings of guilt and regret kept me from using the orbs."

"Yes. I can see how her fears could have affected you in that way. It took me a long time to face my own feelings of guilt as well."

"After a while though, I began to feel as if 'she' was controlling my emotions and I began to hate 'her' self-defeating thoughts and victim mentality. I took a perverse pleasure in virtually rubbing her nose in the events of her past life. For a while, I became both personalities. One, a sadistic torturer named Sulana and the other, the weak and fearful masochistic Tarsia. As I began to use the memory orbs more and more, both personalities started to accept one another and eventually "I" emerged as one."

"That's amazing! It must have taken you a long time to reach that point," Thula commented.

"Yes! And when I reached that point, I realized how much time I had wasted coming to terms with my old persona. That's when I began my new life."

"How exciting Sulana! Please tell me all that has happened since then!" Thula pleaded with anticipation.

"Well, I eventually finished my book on the Rogeston family despite the fact that it didn't add anything new to Zephron Artemus' trilogy. To my surprise, the book did very well, and I earned a lot of money from the royalties. I used that seed money to go back to school, and in a moment of divine inspiration, I decided to study exo-botany and exo-biology and became an expert on both."

"Just like Omega. He'll be so happy to hear that you've chosen his own specialty!" Thula said happily.

"It's what I really wanted to do when I was Tarsia, and I realized that it was still my true love. That, plus Omega's real-life example is what motivated me to go into those fields."

"I remember thinking a long time ago that I had ruined your life by interfering with yours and bringing you here by manipulating events. But I'm glad to hear that eventually it all worked to your advantage," Thula confessed with excitement.

"Now I know in my heart that there are no coincidences in the universe and that our first meeting was all part of the grand scheme of things. You'll be pleased to know that I'm a successfully published exo-botanist and expert on alien biology with several books on the best seller's list and that as a result I've become a multimillionaire!"

"And a pilot as well I see! After your craft landed I expected to see a pilot exit the ship after you stepped onto the tarmac until I realized that you had flown it yourself!" Thula added enthusiastically.

"Yes. After I resolved all my internal conflicts, doors began to open for me, and I took advantage of every opportunity that came my way. I remember how much I enjoyed flying when our father Alexei used to take me up on the Solar Nations II back on Plantanimus. Now, every time I get into the pilot's seat, I think of him with fondness," Sulana said, waxing nostalgic.

"Our father was a great man wasn't he? Perhaps both he and Kani will return to us some day just as you have," Thula said with a smile.

"Anything's possible Thula. But what's important now is that I came back and I'm so glad that I did. I have much more to tell you if you'd care to hear," Sulana said.

"Is the sky blue, do birds fly?! Of course, I want to hear more. I want to hear it all Sulana! C'mon give!" Thula said, laughing and gesturing with her hand.

"Well, you're not the only one that's married and had children, I've also mated. I found a wonderful lizard named Kenard and we're raising a fourteen year old Gulax boy named Kelem!"

Thula brought her hands to her face feeling thrilled with the news. "Where are they, why haven't you brought them here with you?" she asked sounding mildly upset.

"They're on their way here on another transport. They left a week after I did, and as a matter of fact, my parents are coming with them too."

"Sulana are you coming to Centralia to stay here for good?" Thula asked, thinking that it would bring too much joy in her life.

"Yes!" Sulana answered with tears in her eyes. The two women hugged each other feeling that their long cycle of separation was coming to a close.

"Does everyone else know about this but me?" Thula protested, alarmed but happy.

"I'm sorry sister. We all wanted to surprise you, and I felt that it might have driven you crazy waiting for my return during the time that it took to find work for me, my mate and my parents.

So, I asked the others to perpetrate this one last deception for my sake," Sulana said apologetically.

"I should be mad at you and the others, but all I feel is happiness knowing that we're going to be together for a long time!" Thula blurted out happily.

"My mate Kenard is a fantastic historian and Zephron has already found him a position at Centralia U in the History Department. My son Kelem is going to live here at the mansion with us. My parents are moving to the other side of Centralia to finish what's left of the terraforming work on the last ocean, after which they'll retire and live the rest of their days here with us!" Sulana said exultantly.

"We are so fortunate, you and I that we were both able to heal our spirits and carry on with our lives. My life is so full now and I love Elijah and my children with all my heart and soul but you being here is what they used to call in olden times, 'the icing on the cake with a cherry on top'!"

"Great food metaphor sister. As a matter of fact, why don't we go to that booth over there and get us both a sweet treat to celebrate our reunion!" Sulana suggested, pointing to a nearby tent displaying many colorful sugary confections.

The two sisters took each other's hand and ran toward the pastry booth with child-like excitement, much as they once had when they were both young girls on Plantanimus six centuries before.

CHAPTER 14

Alpha Sings for Sulana

The following day Thula and Sulana spent the better part of the morning planning where Sulana, her mate and male offspring would live in the mansion. It was decided with approval of the rest of the family that they would take over Faruk's old apartment which was one of the largest in the mansion and it could easily accommodate Sulana, Kenard and their son Kelem. Faruk had passed away a year before, and his soul now lived in the body of a baby boy born recently to a couple in the colony. Sulana met Thula's children Alexei and Sulana her name sake and was struck at the similarity between them and the first generation of Rogeston children in Plantanimus. Her children were products of a Terran Tarsian mixed marriage as well and they reminded Sulana of her brothers and sisters from that first generation.

From the moment she met the boy and the girl, it was clear to her that they were both kindred souls and that her son Kelem would be a life-long friend with these two children.

In the early afternoon Thula and Sulana were joined by Susan. The three females flew into downtown Landana where they went shopping for things that Sulana's family would need after they arrived, and later they had lunch at one of the fanciest restaurants in the city. Susan and Thula were very impressed with Sulana's piloting skills as well as the plush interior of the craft which Sulana had designed herself.

Later that night after a sumptuous dinner expertly prepared by house services in the main dining room of the mansion, the family remained at the table enjoying a round of pleasant after dinner conversation.

"We have much use for your skills in agriculture and exo-biology Sulana. Have you given any thought as to what specific part of our operation you might want to dedicate yourself to?" asked Waldo, as the food workers were retrieving the last of the dessert plates.

"I'd like to talk to Omega about that. I think that he will have a better feel for whatever direction I should be aiming at. By the way, where is he and when can I see the man? I'm anxious to talk to him after all these years," Sulana inquired.

"Funny you should say that," Waldo answered. "He's up in Zephron's compound. I spoke to the two of them this afternoon and they would like to see you tonight if you want."

"Tonight? Of course I'd like to see them tonight! It's going to be so wonderful reuniting with them and I've missed them so. There's so much that I want to say to the two of them, but especially Omega, for whom I have much to be thankful for."

"Fine we'll all go together," Waldo said addressing the entire table. "We'll have a second round of celebration in your honor Sulana!"

"I'm ready if everyone is," Sulana said, already standing up and looking very excited.

"We'll have to take three flyers," Thula's brother Vardik suggested. "I can take Carlos with me and Sulana and Waldo can split the difference with the rest since both your flyers are bigger."

"Fine. I'll take Susan and Terence and you can take Elijah and Thula on yours," Waldo said addressing Sulana.

Thula's eyes lit up with excitement as she gathered Elijah and Sulana and led them into the main hallway heading towards the back of the mansion.

Ten minutes later, the three flyers were revving up their turbines on the tarmac of the landing field above the garden's waterfall. Sulana could see Waldo's face behind the windshield of his flyer a few meters away and she flashed back to the day twenty-six years before, when she had met him for the first time as a barely pubescent boy pilot of sixteen.

Now she had become a pilot herself and smiled at the thought of flying in formation with the former Kelem Rogeston en route to meet two men who had once long ago existed as Dreamers.

"Watch for downdrafts when you reach the ridge just below the landing pad," Sulana heard Waldo's voice say in her headset.

"Will do," Sulana responded as she pushed the engines' throttle and her ship lifted gently away from the mansion's landing pad. A few dozen meters above the field, Waldo pushed his turbines and climbed up heading toward Zephron's lair one thousand meters above the valley. Sulana followed after him with Vardik bringing up the rear.

Thula could not help but be proud at seeing her once younger sister fly so confidently and expertly in her fancy flyer. She watched with admiration as Sulana operated the controls of the ship with calm concentration.

After the three ships landed, Sulana donned a warm winter coat before opening the cabin's door. She knew that the temperature at this altitude would be much lower than at the bottom of the valley.

Zephron's compound was impressive to say the least. The façade's architecture of the main building resembled an old Greek temple with six large columns supporting a huge porch adorned with capitals at the end of each column. The front doors were massive and were made out of some sort of heavy metal. As the group stepped into the porch, the doors opened, and they were welcomed by a lovely Tarsian woman in her forties whose resemblance to Thula was remarkable.

As soon as she saw Sulana, she walked up to her and gave a warm hug. "Welcome to Mount Olympus Sulana, my name is Matilda." she said with a lovely smile on her Tarsian face.

Sulana remembered that Thula had told her when she'd first arrived twenty six years before that she had grown up with Matilda and had attended the same schools when they were young but she had neglected to tell her that her childhood friend was Thula's virtual clone.

"Thank you Matilda, it's lovely to meet you after all these years."

"Matilda was once Magrit, your next older sister on Plantanimus," Thula whispered in her ear.

Sulana reached for Matilda once again and embraced her remembering her as she was in another life. Her heart could not possibly hold so much happiness all at one time and she had to calm herself, lest she collapse from the joy she was feeling now.

"Come in dear sister. Zephron and Omega can't wait to see you," Matilda said warmly.

Once inside the building, Sulana felt warm enough to take her coat off. They had obviously raised the ambient temperature to make her lizard body comfortable during her visit.

The inside, of the building was modern and did not reflect the Greek motif of its façade. In contrast, the décor was closer to the interior of the old Rogeston compound on Plantanimus rather than Greek revival. Matilda led the group to the center of the place dominated by a large circular living room surrounded by large windows on every side and filled with comfortable couches, sofas and coffee tables, illuminated by four large chandeliers suspended from the ceiling. It reminded Sulana of an old hunting lodge where she had once vacationed with her parents in the Rocky Mountains in old North America back on Earth.

Zephron and Omega appeared at the far end of the room and both walked toward the group with great enthusiasm. Sulana was amazed at Zephron's surprisingly still young appearance and Omega's youthful energy and body language.

They both had aged but not by much. Omega certainly did not look like a man nearing a century of life. His eyes were bright and clear, and his body remained strong and flexible despite the passage of time. Only his head had changed, now being completely bald.

"My dear friend," Sulana said, hugging Omega with tears in her eyes. "I've finally come home. I'm sorry that it took me so long to return to the fold."

"Our moments are but wisps of time in the life of the universe little one," Omega said gently. Sounding like the wise old man that he was.

"You look amazing Omega! I had pictured you in a wheel-chair or at the very least leaning on a cane shuffling along, but your body positively radiates with energy what's your secret?" Sulana asked, truly awed by his physical appearance.

"Good living and a secret or two that I'll tell you about sometime," Omega replied winking.

"You better. Or at this rate you'll outlive us all," Sulana responded laughing.

"I knew this moment would come Sulana. But I'm glad that I'm finally living through it now!" Zephron said, reaching for her and embracing the one Rogeston child that everyone had missed for so long.

"Thank you Zephron. I too am glad that this moment has finally become reality."

Zephron put his arm around Sulana's shoulders and looked at the group. "For the first time in six hundred years, this family is once again whole. Our dear Sulana is with us and all the sadness and pain belongs to the past. This moment…" he said, looking at Sulana with affection. "Is all that we have. The past doesn't exist, and the future is yet to be. So, live in the moment, for the moment is the only reality of consciousness."

Omega brought a tray with glasses of wine and gave one to each person in the group.

"A toast to Sulana to the legacy of the Rogeston family and to the Dreamers, may they live for many eons!" Omega said, raising his glass.

"Here, here!" The group said almost in unison, and then everyone drank from their glasses.

Zephron invited everyone to sit in the center of the living room which consisted of a large round coffee table surrounded by a circular couch. As everyone filed in, Waldo and Omega motioned to Sulana to sit next to them apart from the others.

"Well Sulana, I hear you're a full fleshed botanist and biologist," Omega said after they sat down.

"Yes Om, I'm happy to say. After I returned to Earth I realized that botany was my first love, and following your example, I dove into it with all my might," Sulana replied happily.

Omega and Waldo exchanged glances, and both shifted their weight almost at the same time. Sulana could see that they wanted to discuss something important with her.

"Gentlemen you obviously want to talk to me about something, let's have it!" she said grinning.

"I'll cut to the chase, Sulana. Do you remember our last conversation just before you left for Earth?" asked Waldo.

"How could I ever forget it Waldo? You gave me your and Carlatta's memory orbs as well as Tarsia's and without them I would not have come back when I did. Or perhaps without them I might have never returned."

"Thanks for returning them to us by the way. But that's not the part of the conversation to which I'm referring to now," Waldo said, shaking his head with a smile.

"Oh, I see. You're talking about the seeding of a new generation of Dreamers. How is that coming along by the way?" Sulana asked, looking at both men.

"Quite well actually," Omega interjected, leaning forward and glancing at Waldo momentarily. "We have a prototype growing right up here in Zephron's green house."

Sulana thought she heard wrong and shook her head. "Did you just say that you have a prototype growing up here? And by that, you mean something like a baby Dreamer?"

The two men smiled at each other conspiratorially and looked back at her nodding their heads like two kids who had been bursting to reveal a secret.

Sulana was stunned. She had expected that they would have only developed a basic genetic sequence by now, but not this! "A fully functional living Dreamer?"

"We've named it Alpha and it already thinks and is aware of itself!" Omega said, with pride in his eyes. Waldo nodded in agreement with wide eyes.

"My God you've done it! Sulana said, exhaling as she tried to come to grips with the scope of Omega's accomplishment.

"Yes, we've taken a major step forward, but the project is still in its infancy Sulana. And we're in need of experienced people to reach the next level of development," Waldo added.

"And what would that be?" Sulana asked, wondering what she could possibly contribute to such a difficult undertaking.

"It took us twelve years to grow Alpha. And considering the amount of Dreamers needed to seed so many planets even in ten thousand years, it would take too long for our plan to succeed," Omega said with a worried expression.

"Om, I'm honored that you think that I could bring something to the project. But I'm afraid that you've overestimated my abilities," Sulana said humbly.

"Hmmm, let's see..." Omega said looking up. "You developed a new strain of fast growing cyano-bacteria that could survive the low temperature and acidic soil of Mars. Something that many eminent biologists and bacteriologists had been trying to come up with but had failed to develop for centuries. Your bacteria managed to raise the oxygen content of Mars so fast, that people were able to walk on the surface of Mars with minimum breathing equipment within five years of the seeding of your bacteria. Two years ago, The Martian Terraforming Authority announced that completion of the Mars Terraforming project had been shortened by a decade because of your work. And you accomplished that within five years of graduating from college!" Omega concluded, pointing at her.

"True but..." Sulana began saying and was interrupted by Omega.

"Six years ago, you were involved in the development of an industrial size earth tiller with the capability of removing radioactive contaminated soil from fallow fields that had remained unusable since the Dark Period in the Eurasian territory on Earth. Your contribution was that of developing a new fast acting strain of bacteria that was capable of eating the contaminated soil and excreting normal healthy soil back onto the land," Omega concluded. Spreading his hands triumphantly.

"Okay Om. What's your point?" Sulana said, finally willing to accept his opinion of her capabilities.

"The point I'm trying to make my dear Sulana, is that you seem to have a knack for coming up with ways to accelerate the growth and metabolism of living things! In particular, things that can make terraforming faster and easier, and possibly help in growing more complicated organisms such as a new generation of Dreamers," Omega paused, looking at Sulana briefly with eyebrows raised and then continued. "Your skills precisely match our needs."

Sulana looked at the two men and had to admit that Omega's argument that her knowledge could contribute to the cause made good sense. Her own admiration and respect for the old man's accomplishments had affected her typical high self-esteem.

"We need you Sulana. Not only because of your skills, but because you're the right person for the job. With you along, we can be assured that you can continue working on the project for as long as necessary, building upon each success over time," Waldo added, looking at Sulana with an expectant look.

Sulana understood exactly what Waldo was trying to say with his last statement. Would she be able to commit to the project for more than one life-time? Reincarnation was a subject that she had been debating in her mind for some time now.

"I understand what you're trying to say Waldo. It's something that I have to think about for a while longer before I give you the answer regarding the issue of staying with the project for, 'as long as it takes'," Sulana said accentuating the last words.

"That would be the best of both worlds. But regardless of whether you decide to remain with the project past the ending of your current life or not, we need you now." Omega stated with certainty.

"Count me in. I would be a fool to pass an opportunity to work with you, Omega."

The two men stood up from the couch and rushed over to Sulana, both men hugging her at the same time. They were jubilant and giddy with her answer.

"Can I meet Alpha now?" she asked amidst their excitement.

"Of course!" Omega replied overcome with joy. "Come with us we'll introduce you!"

The three of them got up from the circular couch and excused themselves from the company. Sulana went over Thula to apologize for leaving.

"My dear sister, I knew that these two were going to kidnap you the moment we got up here," Thula said laughing, as she pointed to Waldo and Omega already standing impatiently by a door that obviously led to where Alpha was. "Please don't worry about me we'll have plenty of opportunity to be together."

Sulana reached down and kissed her sister on the forehead and disappeared behind the door with Waldo and Omega.

Omega led Waldo and Sulana down a long corridor which opened to the living area of the complex. A small living room stood in the center with four bedrooms and bathrooms located to the left and right on the second floor of the rear of the house. Behind the living room a door led to a large kitchen with a ceiling full of skylights.

"It must be very bright here during the day," Sulana commented, as she gazed at the night sky through the spacious ceiling.

"Zephron likes a lot of light. I guess it's a leftover from his days as a Dreamer," Waldo said jokingly as he continued walking toward the back of the house.

The rear wall of the kitchen was covered with windows and through them Sulana could see the large dome of a green house a few meters behind a small garden adjacent to the back of the house.

Omega stopped by the door leading to the garden and picked up three knee length coats from a rack sitting next to the kitchen counter.

"You're going to need this," Omega said, handing Sulana one of the coats. "It's even cold for us warm blooded mammals up here."

Omega opened the door and a blast of cold air hit Sulana in the face making her shiver. At night, the temperature in the mountain was several degrees lower than the valley.

Sulana wrapped her arms around her chest and trudged on. She didn't care how cold it was. She was about to meet a living Dreamer for the first time in centuries!

As they walked on the stone path leading to the entrance to the green house, Omega spoke.

"We keep Alpha in a low oxygen environment. When we former Dreamers were growing on Plantanimus, the planet's atmosphere was less than 12% oxygen and we guessed correctly that Alpha would thrive in a similar atmosphere. After we enter through the first pressure door,

I'll hand you each an oxygen canister with a breathing mask, otherwise you'll get dizzy and pass out eventually."

"I won't need one Omega. You forget that we lizards can survive in less oxygen than 12%. When I worked on the surface of Mars I walked around without a breather," Sulana informed him.

"I forgot about your species capacity for processing oxygen so efficiently," Omega acknowledged as they entered through the outer door.

Once inside, Omega handed Waldo an oxygen canister and donned one himself. He turned to Sulana and asked, "are you ready to meet the first living Dreamer to exist in four hundred years?"

Sulana nodded with anticipation, her heart beating fast with excitement.

The door clicked and hissed as it opened slowly and then closed hissing again as the air pumps readjusted the atmosphere inside the dome. The three walked in and stood by the entrance looking at Alpha, as their ears popped adjusting to the change in pressure. Soon, their eyes became accustomed to the low light.

In the middle of the circular dome stood a two-meter-tall mushroom. An exact replica of the fully-grown Dreamers of Plantanimus with a dark greenish cap sitting on a lovely golden stalk, festooned with purple hanging tendrils from the gills beneath its cap. A slight scent of chlorine bleach mixed with apricot hung in the air. The smell transported Sulana to her days as Tarsia and for a moment she thought that she had actually bi-located to the old planet.

"It's something isn't it?" Omega said, with wonder and reverence in his voice.

"It's beautiful Om. You really know how to cook!" Sulana whispered awestruck.

"Do you feel it?" Waldo asked Sulana, pointing to the ground with a smile.

Sulana looked down instinctively but her sensitive ears had already picked up the ultra-low frequency purr emanating from Alpha's body.

"Oh, this brings me back, Omega!" Sulana said, looking at the old man with amazement, and then listening again with a tilt of her head, "by God Omega, he sounds just like you!

"Purely coincidental I assure you," Omega replied, laughing quietly behind his face mask.

"You are after all his father aren't you, Om?" Sulana added, needling him gently.

"Well, I'm teaching him how to sing. After all, a Dreamer must know how to make music and he might have picked up a melody or two from me," he admitted somewhat sheepishly.

"I thought as much," Sulana said smiling widely, still enthralled by the sight of the young seedling. "Can I touch him?"

"You can touch him and talk to him. That's how he communicates with me and Zephron," Omega said matter of fact.

"He talks? How much? she asked, a little surprised.

"He has the intellect of a five-year-old child now. Although I suspect that his IQ will double in the next year or so. He's reached the point in his development where his learning ability will grow exponentially from now on."

Omega pushed Sulana gently forward, assuring her with his expression that it was alright to approach the young Dreamer.

Sulana stepped forward gingerly and stood next to Alpha for a few seconds before placing her hand on his dome. She immediately felt the slight tickle in her hand that had been so familiar to her in her life as Tarsia. It was like the static a person feels when they pass their hands over a woolen garment that has acquired a positive charge, but without the electrical shock.

"HELLO, HOW ARE YOU?" Alpha's words suddenly echoed in her mind.

Sulana gasped and she almost withdrew her hand from Alpha's dome. It had been centuries since she'd experienced this kind of telepathy, and it took some getting used to after such a long time.

"My name is Sulana," she said, half speaking half thinking the words, while at the same time trying to control her emotions.

"YOU'RE DIFFERENT SULANA, ARE YOU A FEMALE?" Alpha asked, sounding like a child.

"Yes Alpha, I'm a female. Do you like females?"

"I LIKE EVERYONE, AND I LIKE YOU AS WELL BUT YOU'RE NOT LIKE THE OTHERS I'VE MET SO FAR," Alpha paused for a second as if struggling to find the right words to say. *"YOU'RE A GULAX! OMEGA TOLD ME ALL ABOUT GULAX AND WHERE THEY CAME FROM AND OTHER THINGS."*

"I see. Well, what do you think of me?" Sulana asked, with a virtual smile in her face.

"WOULD YOU LIKE TO BE MY FRIEND SULANA? I'D LIKE TO BE YOUR FRIEND IF YOU WANT."

"I would very much like to be your friend Alpha."

"AND WILL YOU COME AND VISIT ME EVERYDAY? I GET LONELY SOMETIMES, OMEGA SAID THAT A DREAMER MUST GET USED TO BEING ALONE, BUT I DON'T WANT TO BE ALONE. I LIKE IT WHEN PEOPLE VISIT ME."

"I will come visit you everyday Alpha, I promise," Sulana whispered, as tears of joy began rolling down her cheek.

"YOU FEEL FUNNY SULANA. ARE YOU SAD?" Alpha asked, suddenly sounding worried.

"I'm crying because I'm happy not sad Alpha. I didn't mean to confuse you," Sulana responded, hoping that she wasn't upsetting the young Dreamer.

"I'M NOT CONFUSED. I DON'T WANT YOU TO FEEL SAD BECAUSE OF ME."

"I promise not be sad Alpha you make me happy," Sulana said with a joy in her heart that was deeper than she had ever felt.

"NOW WE'RE BOTH HAPPY. YOU MAKE ME HAPPY ALSO SULANA. I HOPE WE CAN BE FRIENDS FOREVER!" Alpha declared with joy, as Sulana's body began to vibrate sympathetically with the young mushroom.

Alpha began to sing a low note that increased in intensity slowly at first, but then rose in pitch higher and higher until the green house dome began to vibrate to the same frequency as his music.

Just when Sulana's body began to feel as though it would disintegrate with joy and ecstasy, Alpha lowered the intensity of his music and Sulana took a deep breath glad that her atomic structure was still cohesive.

"DID YOU LIKE MY SONG SULANA? I MADE IT JUST FOR YOU."

"Yes, Alpha it was the most beautiful music I've ever heard!" Sulana answered truthfully.

"I'M HAPPY THAT YOU LIKE MY SONG SULANA. BUT SINGING IT MADE ME TIRED. I'M GOING TO DREAM FOR A WHILE, BUT WHEN I WAKE UP, WILL YOU COME TO VISIT ME AGAIN?" Alpha asked, sounding like a sleepy child.

"I will Alpha, I will come back to see you."

"GOODBYE SULANA, IT WAS VERY NICE MEETING YOU." Alpha said, his voice sounding very sleepy now.

"Goodbye Alpha, dream well."

Sulana removed her hand from Alpha's dome and lost her balance almost falling backwards. Fortunately Waldo had walked up behind her and he caught her before she could hit the ground.

Omega came around looking concerned and excited at the same time.

"Bless the Universal Mind God!" Omega said, overcome with emotion. "I never heard Alpha sing like that before! What did you say to him?" He asked with great curiosity.

Sulana still trying to recover from her experience, shook her head. "I don't know. We were just communicating telepathically having what I thought was a normal conversation and then, suddenly he began to sing!"

"Remarkable!" the old man muttered.

"Whatever it was, Alpha really seems to like her!" Waldo said smiling at Omega, as he helped Sulana walk back to the door.

Sulana nodded in agreement.

The trio exited the dome and walked back to the kitchen through the garden. The cool night air brought Sulana back to her normal self, although her mind was still processing what she'd just experienced.

Once inside, they took off their coats and Omega suggested that they all sit at the kitchen table. He quickly boiled a pot of hot water and brewed some green tea which they drank in silence. The two men sensed that Sulana needed some time to deal with the after effects of her 'conversation' with Alpha.

After a few minutes, Sulana put her cup down on the table with force and looked at Omega and Waldo with a focused look in her eyes.

"I thought about it and I've made up my mind," she said with a serious expression.

"What are you referring to?" Omega asked.

"You can count on me to commit to the project for the 'duration,'" Sulana asserted.

Omega slapped his hand on the table top and let out a hoot. "Waldo, you better get those planets terraformed really quick. We're gonna be swimming in baby Dreamers before you know it!

CHAPTER 15

A Warm Summer's Night

The following night Thula and Sulana were sitting on the large terrace facing the garden on the third floor of the mansion. From her lounge chair, Sulana could see the stream that fed the waterfall almost to the point where the water began its journey down to the valley by Zephron's lair near the top of the mountain. The warm summer air carried the scent of alfalfa and strawberries from the farm fields to the south. The scent mixed with the sweet smell of all the exotic flowers in the garden below.

It was one dash three past midnight and the mansion was quiet. Everyone had gone to sleep but Sulana's mind was too stimulated to fall asleep. Her encounter with Alpha made her realize what it was that she was supposed to do for the rest of her life and beyond. Her decision to commit to the project opened up a gate of ideas in her mind and after trying to sleep for over an hour she gave up and sneaked down to the basement kitchen to fix herself a midnight snack. Perhaps with a full stomach she might doze off eventually.

When she reached the kitchen, she found Thula there trying to remedy the same problem. They laughed at the coincidence and after fixing two large plates of food they decided to come up to the terrace and talk for a while as they ate their food al fresco.

"I haven't been able to sleep well since you arrived," Thula admitted as she chewed on a grilled carrot.

"I know what you mean. I haven't slept more than four or five hours in the last two days and after meeting Alpha I may never close my eyes again!"

"Isn't he wonderful Sulana? I can't believe that we have a Dreamer living amongst us once again," Thula commented with wonder. "We owe Omega a debt of gratitude."

"Is it my perception, or has Omega become the de facto head among the former Dreamers having higher status that Zephron himself?" Sulana asked.

"No, it's not just your perception. I think that you're right. Omega is second only to Waldo in this current cycle," Thula concurred. Then, turning to face Sulana she added, "you've been away from us for a long time. In the future, as you return from each former life, you'll learn that your previous position and status within the colony will have changed, mainly because each time you return, you must go through childhood and adolescence. And no matter how mature you may be by the age of five or six, you'll still be considered a child by the rest of us."

"I can't say I look forward to that!" Sulana retorted.

"After two or three re-incarnations, you'll get used to it!" Thula said laughing.

"What a crazy world!" Sulana said, raising her glass of juice to the stars, joining her sister in laughter.

The two women talked for a while telling each other funny stories from their past catching up on the minutiae of twenty six years of separation. After a while, they became quiet sitting next to each other enjoying the warm summer night while looking at the bright stars in the Centralian sky.

"You never finished explaining what it was that changed your mind about coming back," Thula said, breaking the silence.

"You're right, I didn't." Sulana stood up, then she walked over to the terrace's railing and leaned on it with her back to the garden.

"About nine years ago my Kenard and Kelem went to the Sahara on a father son male bonding camping adventure. It was Kenard's way of teaching a young Gulax boy how to survive in a desert environment. Something about "getting in touch with the Gulax inside" Sulana said laughing. "They were never more than two or three kilometers from the nearest town, but I suppose it made them feel like real lizards pretending that they were in the middle of the Tak desert on Gulax Prime!"

"Boys will be boys!" Thula commented laughing.

"Exactly! Anyway, they were gone for a few days and that week I was on sabbatical from Johannesburg U. And having nothing to do, I turned on my vid-wall to pass the time. I was flipping channels looking for something worthy to watch, when I happened to stumble on the original film version of James Hilton's Lost Horizon. I always liked that film even though it was ancient and had been photographed in black and white and was two dimensional to boot. But something about that era of film making always appealed to me, and so I decided to watch it."

Thula got up from her chair and joined Sulana on the railing drawn by Sulana's anecdote.

"After I finished watching the film I began to cry as I had never cried before. I became hysterical because I was crying and the more I cried the more upset I became! I thought I was going to have a nervous breakdown even though lizards don't do such things! And then it hit me square in the face!"

"What hit you square in the face?" Thula asked, with curious interest.

"The realization that I was Robert Conway, the lead character in James Hilton's story!" Sulana said with a sad expression.

Thula tilted her head not understanding the point of Sulana's story.

"Do you remember us talking about Shangri La a few hours before I succumbed to my psychic coma twenty six years ago?" Sulana said, reminding Thula of that moment in time.

"Of course!" Thula said, now remembering that conversation years before, realizing what Sulana was driving at.

"You can see the similarities in the two narratives can't you? Sulana asked rhetorically.

"Yes, I see what you mean," Thula agreed.

"I realized to my chagrin that I had found paradise here in Centralia, and just like the foolish Robert Conway character, I too had walked out of Shangri La because of ignorance and fear."

"Yes, but just like Robert Conway you came back and found your Shangri La once again!" Thula said her voice full of emotion.

"I did indeed sister. And you were a big part of the reason for my return."

"Welcome back Sulana. No matter where we each might go from now on, we'll never be apart again," Thula said, feeling that a great burden had been removed from their lives.

With eyes full of tears the two women embraced and held each other, feeling the deep love of family in their hearts.

Even though Sulana had been back for two days, it was only now at this moment that the two women felt a sense of closure and the healing of the wounds caused by the long years spent apart from each other. Both finally understood that the suffering they had endured through the centuries had more to do with the reconciliation of their spirits rather than the separation caused by time and distance.

Without saying a word, they bid each other goodnight and Thula went back to her room. Sulana stayed behind and turned around to look up at the mountain once again. She marveled at the history of the Rogeston family dating back to the 23rd century on Earth when humans were recovering from the Dark Period. A time when humanity had almost perished because of greed and lack of concern for the environment. From the days of Dr. Isaac Mallory Rogeston in 2252 and Eve Marchant to Kelem Rogeston, the bloodline had produced a prodigious number of important figures dotting the history of the human race. Now, she finally felt her spiritual connection to the family and realized that she had a place in the narrative of their story.

She thought of Alpha and the incredible sensation she experienced linking telepathically with the young seedling the night before and knew in her heart that she would become his caretaker from now on. She knew at last that her destiny was to ensure that the legacy of Plantanimus would never be forgotten.

One day soon, not too long from now, the universe would be filled with the sweet music of the Dreamers once again…

THE END

Thank you for reading Reunion. The next and last book of the pentalogy is titled, **The Holographic Saint**. It is the fifth and final chapter of the Plantanimus/Kelem Rogeston saga which takes place in the year 10,023.

About the Author

A resident of Los Angeles California, Joseph M. Armillas is an author, actor and film producer. Born in South America to show business parents and raised in the USA, Joseph is a US Army veteran and proud American. A science fiction fan since childhood, Joseph began writing short sci-fi stories while in high school. His love of the genre inspired him to write the Plantanimus Pentalogy. He is currently working on converting the five books into screenplays.

Printed in the United States
By Bookmasters